STI

"There!" She pointed at the stone floor in front of the worktable.

Andrea quickly went to the crumpled body of Deborah Foley. Her white wool dress was twisted around her legs just below the knees. The broken glass of the ether bottle lay around her. Blood from a deep cut on the underside of her thigh had soaked and spread through the woolen fibers of her dress, creating a surreal pattern. Another cut on her upper arm had bled onto the floor, discoloring the stones.

"Oh, God. She's dead. I knew it the minute I saw her."

"No, she isn't! There's still a pulse." Andrea shouted, "Now get the hell out of here and get some help!"

——————————— ★ ———————————

"Carolyn Coker strikes again . . . Andrea Perkins, the beautiful American art restoring sleuth, tackles what may be her most scintillating mystery yet . . ."

—*Publishers Weekly*

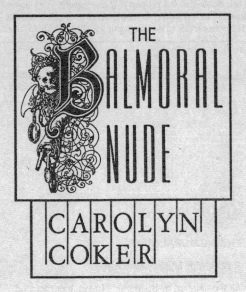

THE BALMORAL NUDE

CAROLYN COKER

W✪RLDWIDE®

TORONTO • NEW YORK • LONDON
AMSTERDAM • PARIS • SYDNEY • HAMBURG
STOCKHOLM • ATHENS • TOKYO • MILAN
MADRID • WARSAW • BUDAPEST • AUCKLAND

THE BALMORAL NUDE

A Worldwide Mystery/March 1993

First published by St. Martin's Press, Incorporated.

ISBN 0-373-28002-5

For the cousins Judy, Ruth, Carlyse, and Annabelle

PROLOGUE

London—1864

WILLIAM EWART GLADSTONE, the chancellor of the exchequer, informed the police that Emma had been murdered.

The death of a prostitute by deliberate malice was not uncommon in London's West End. Among the frequenters of the local gin shops, such an occurrence would merit little more than a passing mention. Beyond that, murder was usually dismissed as being a crime of passion and, because of its suddenness, perhaps less to be abhorred than a more lingering death from disease or starvation.

Still, Emma's murder was remarked upon more than most because of "him wot done it, and him wot seen it done."

The captain at the Bow Street police station was as startled as the gin shop regulars by the identity of the witness, the aforementioned Gladstone, and the accused, Cecil Thomas Fetherston, a successful artist and owner of the Fetherston Art Gallery.

The police captain, being a man of ambition, routinely read the *Times* and the *Spectator* to keep abreast of the happenings in The City and to familiarize himself with the activities of influential men who might be helpful to his career. For this reason, he recognized the name of the chancellor as well as that of the artist.

Only a few days earlier the *Times* reported that Fetherston had returned from Balmoral Castle in Scotland, where he had spent the previous month as art consultant and private tutor to Her Majesty, Queen Victoria. The newspaper report was accompanied by an editorial to the effect that such activity undoubtedly served in some measure to relieve the queen's grief at the loss of her beloved prince consort, Albert. However, the editorial continued, three years had passed since her husband's death, and it was time for the queen to put down her paintbrush and pick up her scepter. There was "danger in indulging in the luxury of sorrow."

"Are you sure it was Fetherston who done the girl in?" The captain glared at the arresting officer. "We wouldn't want it said that we arrested the wrong man."

"There's no mistake, sir." The young bobby reddened. He had brought in a confession that Fetherston wrote out himself and signed of his own free will. What else could the captain want?

"I won't have my men using coercion," the captain said sternly. "You can't let your zeal run away with you."

"There was nothing like that at all, sir. He came along as pretty as you please. 'I suppose you've come about Emma,' he says, before I so much as opened my mouth."

"Where did you run him down?"

"No running to it," the young policeman continued. "He was waiting for us right there in his art gallery—it's in the same building as the gin shop. Standing at an easel, he was, drawing a picture. And when I told him that I was there to ask him a few questions about Emma, he took down the paper he'd been drawing on and put it in amongst a lot of other drawings in a bloody big folder—''

The captain frowned at the vulgarity.

"Sorry, sir.'' The younger man stood silent a moment in embarrassment.

"Continue.''

"Yes, sir. He put the picture in a big folder, put the folder on a shelf in a cabinet and put on his coat. 'No point in hanging about,' he says, 'you may as well take me on to the station house.' ''

The police captain thumped the edge of his desk with two flattened fingers. Then, shaking his head, he picked up the brief confession and read it again. It was straightforward enough. No margin of doubt.

Well, if Fetherston was determined to get himself hanged because of some little whore who kept a room above a gin shop, that was his concern.

"Now tell me, son''—the captain nodded toward a chair next to his desk—"sit down and tell me what part Mr. Gladstone had in all of this.''

The young policeman gratefully accepted the invitation to sit, though he still kept his shoulders erect and his knees and ankles pressed squarely together. After some prompting from the captain, a story emerged that had not been committed to paper in the written report.

"I had stopped on my nightly rounds in front of the Copping Street gin shop to chat with two of the girls. Always good for a smile, those two are—but nothing else,'' the constable hurried to assure the captain.

"Go on.''

"The girls were laughing and showed me pamphlets that Mr. Gladstone had given them about saving their souls and repenting before God and suchlike. Most of the girls in that neighborhood know who he is. Look on him as a joke, most of them do. 'He can tell *others* that it's our souls he's after,' the girls say, 'but we know why he comes here on his nighttime walkabouts.' "

"Yes, well. Get on with your story."

"As myself and the two girls were standing there, a gentleman comes running down the outside stairway from the second-story rooms. He was holding his shirt together with one hand, and the other hand was pressed against the side of his head. Blood was oozing out between his fingers. He started off, stumbling on his shoelaces, in the direction of Covent Garden. I was set to go after him when Mr. Gladstone came out on the landing at the top of the stairs. 'Constable,' he shouted—loud-like, but not urgent, if you know what I mean—'up here,' he says, 'there's been a mishap.' "

"A mishap?"

"That's what he said, sir."

The captain covered his mouth with his hand and coughed. "Go on," he said.

"Mr. Gladstone turned back," the policeman leaned forward in his chair, "I ran up the stairs and followed him down the hall. The third door on the left was open, and Emma—the deceased—a girl of about eighteen, was sprawled nude on the bed. A knife—not precisely a knife—a scraper, more like, a thin-bladed paint scraper was protruding from her breast and had penetrated her rib cage."

"So the man who ran down the stairs was Fetherston?"

"No, sir. I didn't get that gentleman's name." The young policeman took a wadded handkerchief from his pocket and pressed it between his hands. "The way Mr. Gladstone explained it, Emma had taken a man—someone she met in the gin shop—upstairs to her room.

They had been in bed for—a while—when Fetherston knocked on the door. Emma didn't answer. Fetherston flung open the door, and when he saw the two of them together, he went crazy. He had the sharp instrument in his hand. The two men scuffled, but the stranger managed to escape. He's the one with the open shirt and bloodied head I saw coming down the stairs."

"Why did Fetherston kill the woman?"

The young policeman studied the crumpled handkerchief between his hands. "He was in love with her, sir."

The captain laughed; or that was what it sounded like, but his face was as stern as before.

"Fetherston was in love with Emma," the constable said again, not sure that the captain had heard him. "That's what the Copping Street girls said."

"And that's why he killed her?"

"Yes, sir."

Rain splattered against the window, and the captain stood to watch as though it were an unknown phenomenon in London. After a moment, he turned back toward the room. "And Fetherston was gone by the time you got there?"

"Yes, sir. He went down the inside stairs through the gin shop and straight back to his studio. He didn't even try to get away."

"And he agreed to make a confession without any argument?"

"Yes, sir."

"We won't need any more evidence than that. There's no need to mention Mr. Gladstone in your report."

"Whatever you say, sir."

The captain did not say anything more at the moment.

It was an open secret that William Gladstone prowled the nighttime streets of the West End. Social work, he called it. There was at least one known attempt to blackmail him for accosting prostitutes. He had not denied that he had done so. Indeed, he had acknowledged it with the singularly bland comment that his actions were "certainly not within the rules of worldly prudence."

Gladstone, the police captain knew, would most certainly be prime minister sooner or later. He was especially popular among the working people. As chancellor of the exchequer he had reduced income tax. And though the rich were growing richer, the poor were not quite as poor. With such a promising political career ahead of him, no doubt he would be grateful if his name was not linked with tonight's incident. The captain opened the middle drawer of the desk and put the report inside.

"What I don't understand," he said before dismissing the constable, "is what Gladstone's role was in all this."

"He claims he was an eyewitness, sir."

"How the bloody hell"—vulgarity was not off limits to the captain, only to his subordinates—"could he be a witness to something that happened in a room where the door was closed?"

"I wondered about that, too, at first."

"Well?"

"When I went back for a second look, I noticed there was a closet in Emma's room that had a curtain in front of it. There was a chair in there. And on the floor beside it, I found a pamphlet like the ones the girls from Copping Street showed me."

"Jesus."

"Yes, sir."

"Do you think he was in—?"

"I didn't like to ask him, sir." The young officer rolled the handkerchief into a small ball between the palms of his hands. "By then I already had a signed confession."

"Right."

"I mean, him being the chancellor of the exchequer and all..."

"Right. You were quite right."

"And all his preaching against sin..." The constable left the rest of his explanation unspoken.

For a moment, the only sound was the rain pelting against the window.

Then, there was no mistaking it. It was not a cough this time but a laugh, although the captain's face bore no signs of humor. "I guess it's not a sin," he said, "if all you do is watch."

THE CAPRICIOUSNESS of death is always startling. It is tempting to look for patterns, but it is useless to try.

More than one hundred years after the brutal death of Emma, the Copping Street prostitute, the names of Cecil Fetherston, William Gladstone, and Queen Victoria were once again linked with tragedy.

In 1864, Fetherston was tried for murder, found guilty, and executed. Gladstone survived until 1898, four years after completing his fourth term as prime minister. Queen Victoria led Great Britain out of the nineteenth century and died in 1901 at the age of eighty-two. But their paths crossed again, posthumously, in the late twentieth century and the result—again—was murder.

ONE

THE GIRL FROM the British Tourist Authority probably would have gotten back home alive if she had worn her old Burberry raincoat instead of the new plaid blazer.

She had wavered between the two. The argument for the raincoat was that the beginning drizzle could easily escalate into all-out rain. The blazer scored the winning points, however, because the nipped-in style emphasized her small waist and the rust-colored stripe complemented her red hair. On an ordinary day, practicality would have won. But today was not ordinary. This morning she was scheduled to deliver copies of the new "Prestige Travel Map" to the concierge at Claridge's. She always tried to look her best when she called in at a posh hotel. One could never tell who might be passing through the lobby.

What would you do, she asked herself, if you *did* meet someone interesting?

She was almost thirty, and recently this sort of annoying question popped into her head more and more often. She'd probably close up like some great sea mollusk and slither away, she admitted. But the blazer should at least distinguish her from the wallpaper.

She turned the collar of the new jacket up in the back for a casual effect—the way it had been displayed on the mannequin in the window of Marks and Spencer— thought better of it, and smoothed the collar down again. In a last-minute concession to being "sensible" she stuffed a plastic head scarf into her briefcase, then double-locked her small flat and ran to the corner to hail a taxi.

By the time the cab pulled up in front of Claridge's, the drizzle had stopped, as though gathering strength for a more impressive display. Accumulated moisture dripped from a giant Union Jack directly above the front door. The British flag hung from a brass pole attached at an angle to the facade of the hotel. It was flanked by the flags of the United States, Denmark, Canada, West Germany, Italy, and France. When the wind lifted and flourished the waterlogged banners, a sort of international rain fell on the brass overhang above the entrance and dripped through the lacy metal trim around the edges onto the sidewalk.

"Careful of the drip," the doorman warned again and again as he held a large, black umbrella above the heads of guests and propelled them in or out of their taxis. His portal-to-portal routine had the same easy grace as that of a professional host at the latest nostalgic resurrection, the Sunday afternoon Tea Dance.

Taxi door—step, step, turn.

Hotel door—step, step, turn.

Taxi door—step, step, turn.

The girl in the blazer grabbed her briefcase from the seat beside her. The doorman escorted her across the sidewalk and returned to open the door of the taxi that pulled into the vacated spot at the curb. A gray-haired couple in rumpled Irish tweeds got out.

Next to arrive was a tall man in a light brown cashmere jacket. He clutched an eight-by-ten manila envelope to his chest and hunched forward slightly to protect it from water spots. Once inside, he hurried to the far side of the crowded lobby.

The doorman's rhythm was thrown off by the next arrival, who loitered in the cab—purposely, it seemed—adjusting the hood of a zippered jogger's jacket and putting on a pair of totally unnecessary sunglasses.

Dark glasses in place, the jogger entered the lobby and made for a vacant red-leather chair in a small dark alcove under the curved stairway that led to the mezzanine.

"I'm sure the queen wouldn't approve of *that*," a woman with an American Airlines carry-on bag slung across her mink-coated shoulder said.

"What?" Her husband, like most of the guests who were concerned only with their own arrivals or departures, had not noticed the offensive breach in acceptable attire.

"Or Mrs. Thatcher, for that matter. They both come here sometimes to state dinners. It says so in the brochure. What do you suppose *they'd* think if they saw someone in running shoes lounging in the lobby of Claridge's?"

The woman's husband squinted in the direction of the jogger and noticed only the incongruity of the sunglasses. "Probably from California," he said, hustling his wife toward the exit.

Though there was a reading lamp on a small desk in the alcove, it was not turned on and the shadows under the stairway provided anonymity. Across the room, however, the man with the manila folder was anything but inconspicuous. Clayton Foley could not have gone unnoticed if he tried. At six feet five, he was a head taller than anyone else in the lobby. In America, strangers who saw him in a crowd usually thought he looked familiar. Some were sure they had seen his face at close range before—maybe in a locker-room interview on television. In England, at academic dinners or receptions, he often was pegged as an American chap who had studied at Oxford on a Rhodes scholarship. His field of study—someone would say they remembered—had been art history of the Victorian era. At Harrods, women shoppers who saw him in the midst of a jumble of klieg lights and photographic equipment thought they recognized him as the model for the Harris Tweed ads in fashion magazines. All three conclusions were correct.

Clayton Foley stood, now, looking around for the person he had come to meet. Finally, as his glance came to the desk of the concierge, he spotted the back of a familiar-looking plaid jacket and an abundance of copper-colored hair. With the hint of a grin on his face, he started in that direction. His long stride could have been interpreted as a swagger. In fact, the swing of his shoulders was to compensate for a left knee that refused to bend the way it used to.

The concierge was on the phone with a car rental agency on behalf of one of the guests who had specified a four-door Vauxhall, not a coupé.

Spread out on the counter in front of him were a number of Prestige Travel Maps that had been delivered by the girl from the Tourist Authority. She stood self-consciously waiting for his attention to return. Just as she busied herself looking into her briefcase once more, Clayton Foley grabbed her and held her motionless in front of him, clasping her back against his chest. Above her head a deep voice rumbled, ''Hi, Red! What'll it be—the dining room, or your room?''

The girl gasped in surprise. Foley's arms unlocked and his large hands found her elbows and spun her around. She looked up at him with something approaching terror. In an instant his smile was gone and his expression was as startled as her own.

"Sorry. Wrong redhead," Foley said. "I thought you were someone else."

The girl took an instinctive step backward, knocking her briefcase to the floor. Pamphlets, brochures, photographs, and manila envelopes spilled around their feet.

"It was the hair and that jacket. She used to have a jacket like that." Foley stooped uncomfortably, favoring his left knee, and helped her retrieve the scattered papers.

Without speaking, the girl scooped the spilled contents back into her briefcase.

"Wait! That one's mine." Foley laughed and retrieved his envelope from among the girl's. "Again, I apologize," he said, then turned back toward the lobby.

Still flustered, the girl stacked the maps she had delivered in a neat pile on the desk. She glanced at the tall man who had already turned away from her to search the lobby for that other girl who once had a blazer like hers.

She told herself that it was exactly as he had said, a case of mistaken identity—something to laugh about. It was an incident that had called for a clever remark on her part, a remark that he would have found so amusing that he would want to see her again. How many novels, how many magazine articles had she read where the lovers met in a situation like this? Lasting relationships started that way.

But no clever phrase flew to her lips. Nothing came to mind—not even a soothing maxim to cool the blush that burned her cheeks. The shyness that was as much a part of her as the color of her hair burned in her throat like a flu virus. All she could think of was how to get away as quickly as possible.

The concierge was still involved on the telephone. She waved at him and pointed to the stack of maps she had left, then turned to leave. Head bent as though she were absorbed in thoughts of her next pressing engagement, she hurried away.

The jogger in the shadowed alcove stood quickly. There was a choice to be made: follow the girl or stick with Clayton Foley. Foley still had a manila envelope, but was it the same one? Had there been a switch? Foley was meeting someone here. He would stay put for a while. But if the girl got away, this opportunity might be lost forever.

Weaving past clusters of tourists and stacks of luggage, the jogger followed the route the girl had taken. A streak of rust-and-gray plaid was visible through the glass of a revolving door ahead. The girl turned when she reached the sidewalk. The jogger was close behind.

"Miss!"

The girl paused. There was a tremulousness, an expectancy about her expression when she turned to look back. At first she thought—hoped—it was the man who had grabbed her in the lobby. Seeing instead a hooded figure wearing dark glasses in the gray half-rain, she began to walk even faster toward the corner. She cut across the narrow side street heading toward Grosvenor, where taxis from all areas of Mayfair converged before lining up in front of Claridge's.

"Hey, lady!" The rubber-soled running shoes made squishing sounds against the wet sidewalk. "I think you've got something that doesn't belong to you!"

Frantically, the girl stopped at the curb and raised her hand, waving at one of the careening taxis that skidded around the corner. That pause—just long enough to hail a cab—allowed the jogger to catch up with her.

Slick, wet fingers grabbed her briefcase. "Give me that envelope and then we can both get out of the rain."

In a reflex action, the girl tugged back at the briefcase. "Stop! Stop it!"

Still not fully recovered from the incident in the lobby with the stranger, she was suddenly terrified. For God's sake, what did they want with her? There was nothing in the briefcase worth protecting: maps and brochures and the plastic head scarf she had been in too big a hurry to put on. But just as someone escaping from a burning building often finds he has risked his life to save a stack of worthless Playbills or carried out the everyday flatware and left the sterling behind, she refused to let go.

The uneven stones of the sidewalk were wet and slippery, and the thin leather soles of her high-heeled shoes afforded her little traction. Her hands were wet, too, making it fairly easy to jerk the briefcase out of her fingers.

All her energy had been concentrated in pulling away from the hooded thief. With the briefcase gone, there was no longer any resistance to hold her. She stumbled backward into the street.

The cab driver could not have avoided her. That was never even suggested. Witnesses corroborated his story that it would have been impossible to stop in time. It looked as though the girl in the plaid blazer had simply lost her footing and fallen into the street.

No one mentioned the jogger. Those who were questioned said they had been going about their own business until they heard the scream and turned to look.

It was not the scream that the cab driver would remember for the rest of his life. It was the thud against
the bumper, and the lurching and bumping of first the
front tires, then the back, as they rolled over the ob-
struction in the road before he could bring the taxi to a
halt.

TWO

THE SOUND of the ambulance's arrival on Davies Street went unnoticed in the lobby of Claridge's. The siren's warning was buffered by the hotel's double doors and perforated by the spiky voices of arriving and departing guests until it became no more insistent than the ping of the elevator bell.

Clayton Foley looked through the crowd again. Andrea Perkins obviously had not yet arrived. He found it damned annoying to be put in the position of peering into the face of everyone who came through the door. He remembered Andrea as always being punctual.

It had been almost seven years since they had seen each other. And even though she had hesitated when he telephoned and asked her to meet him, he could not believe that she would take their reunion lightly.

There were no available chairs left in the lobby. After several minutes he chose an inconspicuous spot near the entrance and leaned against the paneled wall. He had mastered the technique of appearing perfectly at ease while keeping his shoulders straight and his stomach flat. To enhance this effect, he seemed to be studying the address on the large envelope he held. No one who might recognize him from the Harris Tweed ads on the sides of buses or in Harrods' winter catalog would guess that he was being kept waiting.

Andrea was not deliberately late. She had left her small hotel in Bloomsbury in plenty of time. Nor was the taxi to blame for the delay. The driver took the most direct route to Mayfair down Oxford Street and, as it happened, straight into a traffic jam created by the ambulance and police cars near Claridge's.

"Sorry, Miss. It looks like a bloody big mix-up ahead." The cab just managed to swerve on to a side street. "I'll go back to Regent Street and try to come in on Grosvenor."

"Never mind. I can walk from here." Andrea dug into her new canvas tote bag for the fare. The tote bag had *Firenze* stenciled in green on the side ("So you'll remember where to come back to," Aldo Balzani had said when he gave it to her on the way from Florence to the nearest airport, in Pisa). It held her cherished art implements, an umbrella, a comb, a hand mirror, two shades of lipstick, and, beneath a bundle of paint-brushes—one sable, one red sable, one ox hair, one camel hair, and three different sizes of flat bristles—her billfold.

She thanked the driver, then made a small leap onto the sidewalk over the dirty stream of water slushing down the drain next to the curb. There was a light drizzle, but not enough to warrant opening the umbrella. As she reached the corner, she saw a group of people huddled close together behind the metal tubing of a barricade that had been set up to block off the street. At the feet of the crowd, she could see warning flares fuming and spewing their deep-pink flames. Above the onlookers' heads were flashes of red from the revolving light on the ambulance. Andrea caught a glimpse of a taxicab parked at an angle in the middle of the street. The driver, looking dazed, was slumped against the dented front bumper. He absently pulled pieces of broken glass from the frame around the headlight and dropped them to the ground.

Andrea's view of the scene opened up when the woman in front of her took the arm of the man she was with and leaned her head against his shoulder. For the first time, she saw the body of a young woman lying in the street. The head, with its tangled, reddish hair, was bent strangely forward. The face was hidden beneath the turned-up lapel of a gray-and-rust plaid jacket. Andrea had the strange impression of a swan with its head beneath its wing. As two uniformed attendants ordered the crowd to disperse, a third crew member collected a mud-smeared briefcase and some crumpled brochures from the sidewalk.

Andrea's stomach lurched and she quickly looked away, not wanting to know any more about the accident than she had already seen. Many of those people behind the barricade, Andrea thought, would stand and watch until the last shard of broken headlight and the last drop of blood were cleaned from the pavement. And yet, she knew she shared a part of their morbid fascination. Though she felt grief and pity for the unknown woman, there was also a sense of relief that the disaster had nothing to do with her or anyone she knew.

She hurried on toward Claridge's, trembling and feeling slightly ill. She wished Aldo were there so he could put his arm around her and say something comforting in his Louisiana drawl.

Aldo Balzani was the man Andrea loved probably more than anyone else in the world. Though he was born in Italy, where most of his family still lived, Aldo had grown up in the home of his grandmother in New Orleans. His mother had died before he was old enough to form a memory of her. After his graduation from Tulane, he went to Florence to visit his policeman father with every intention of using the return portion of his airline ticket. But he had been warmed by the attention and affection of the countless Balzani relatives. A large family with its private jokes and shared concerns was a new and pleasant experience. Finally, he gave in to his father's urgings to stay and join him in the police department.

Andrea had met Aldo—a chief of detectives—when she was serving a one-year apprenticeship as assistant to the curator of the Galleria dell'Accademia in Florence. Aldo was investigating a scam involving a plan to steal and counterfeit a painting purported to be by Michelangelo, and Andrea's art expertise had proved crucial.

The streetlight turned green as Andrea reached the corner, but she was stopped at the curb by the warning siren of a late-arriving police car speeding through the intersection toward the scene of the accident. She wished she had not seen the girl's body.

One of the amazing things about Aldo was that though he dealt with tragedy on a daily basis, he still kept his equilibrium. He could laugh and sing and make love with great enthusiasm as though he did nothing more emotionally draining than—like his Italian uncles and cousins—produce fruit-flavored gelato for a living.

She missed Aldo and wished he were with her. Then why, she asked herself with a small pang of guilt, was she hurrying to meet Clayton Foley?

She *always* tried to be on time for appointments, she told herself, it was nothing more than that. At any rate, being late to meet Clayton Foley was, in a sense, the meting out of justice; retribution in tiny measure. After all, how often had he kept her waiting? There was no way to calculate, and she told herself, no point, either. Like millions of other college romances theirs had been shot through with broken dates. Granted, Clayton always had a perfectly acceptable excuse for being late—except that last time. Disappearing for an entire weekend with a girl from Radcliffe had not been acceptable. Of course, that wasn't what he told Andrea. The *facts* were presented to her haltingly—but with a degree of malicious pleasure—by a fellow student at the Harvard School of Fine Arts. "This is not just gossip, Andrea. I don't believe in gossip. But as your friend, I have to tell you...Clayton and this girl I know..." It had gone something like that.

Andrea had felt hurt, disappointed; she had grieved. But it was not as though they had been lovers, though there was no question about Clayton's intentions. And Andrea had begun to think that was what she wanted, too. But before she had made a decision, the girl from Radcliffe interfered. Ultimately, Andrea had accommodated the disappearance of Clayton Foley from her life easily enough. The loss was like a shiny lacquer wiped from a smooth surface which, once gone, leaves no trace, or almost no trace. It was natural, she told herself, to wonder what it would have been like. And now, hearing from him again after almost seven years was a surprise, nothing more. She was curious. That was all.

At the entrance of the hotel, the doorman ushered Andrea in with a half bow as he held the door. Life had gone on undisturbed at Claridge's.

As she crossed the carpet and started up the short steps into the lobby, there was a moment of adjustment between the chill of the gray day outside and the warmth of the hotel's interior. The hum of conversation was a cheerful mix of laughter and happy exclamations. The scent of expensive perfume, damp fur, and wet wool combined to make an altogether comforting and pleasant atmosphere.

"There you are!" Clayton Foley had his hands on her shoulders before she realized he was there. Looking into her face, he said, "You haven't changed—maybe a little. You're more gorgeous than ever. Here. Let's check that wet raincoat."

Clayton had not changed, either. He had taken charge, peeling off her coat and motioning for the bell captain before she had said a word.

"Do you want to check the bag, too?"

"No, I'll keep it with me." She never entrusted the bag of art implements to strangers. No one but she recognized their value.

"I had a great opening line," Clayton said, "but I've already used it on some girl with hair the same color as yours."

With the coat disposed of and the claim check in his pocket, Clayton took Andrea's arm and guided her toward the dining room.

"Was she impressed?"

"Who?"

"The girl you mistook for me. The one who got to hear your terrific opening line."

"No. She looked at me like I was some vile miscreant and ran for the exit."

"You didn't used to resort to terrifying women to get their attention."

"Maybe it's the language barrier. Sometimes the British don't understand English."

The maître d' greeted them in cordial, subdued tones and directed them to a linen-covered table set with Royal Doulton china.

"I hope this was a convenient place to meet," Clayton said as a waiter silently appeared at his elbow. "They always do up breakfast pretty well here."

"Yes, fine."

Andrea, like most American visitors to England, had long ago decided that breakfast was the better part of British cuisine and did not object when Clayton ordered the full complement for each of them. It included plump sausages, salty kippers, lean slices of bacon, succulent lamb chops, poached eggs, broiled tomatoes, thin wedges of dry toast lined up in a silver rack, crystal compotes of Hampshire butter and orange marmalade.

"And a pot of coffee instead of tea." Clayton handed the menu back to the attentive waiter.

When he had gone, Andrea took the obvious path to conversation. "Tell me again how you knew I was in London. It all sounded so vague over the telephone. And you didn't really explain what *you're* doing here, for that matter."

Clayton gave her one of his photogenic smiles. "Yes. Well, let's *do* talk about me first."

"We always did."

Clayton laughed. He never disguised his ego. That was part of his charm. He was openly and unabashedly interested in himself and his well-being above anything else. And—a little warning buzzer went off in Andrea's head—if you hung around Clayton long enough, you began to think maybe he was justified.

"After I finished at Cambridge, I just never went back across the herring pond—as my obnoxious late father-in-law insisted on calling the Atlantic Ocean. Now, since my wife inherited the family manor in the Cotswolds that's our permanent address."

The waiter arrived with a trolley loaded with silver-domed dishes, which he uncovered and arranged on the table. Then, like the steam released from the plates, he disappeared.

"Fortunately, thank God, because I'm such a handsome devil and in great demand to sell scratchy wool jackets to people who ride buses and leaf through catalogs, I have to spend a lot of time in London. So, we've taken a flat in Bayswater."

"You and what's-her-name from Radcliffe?"

"No, the second Mrs. Clayton Foley and I."

"Oh? Is your wife here with you now?"

"Neither my wife nor anyone else's." He leaned forward and spoke in a growling whisper—and at the same time, rubbed his ankle against hers under the table—"so if you're at loose ends, pretty lady, I can fit you in until the end of the week."

Andrea's anger was like flash paper—igniting in an instant. How *dare* he? She was making a concession just *seeing* him again. If he had gone through that routine on the telephone about needing her professional help just so he could make a pass... And then she heard him laugh and realized that she had been set up.

"You bastard," she said vehemently. In a moment she was giggling like—probably like she had not since the last time she saw Clayton Foley.

"Yeah," he agreed, in a one-word, self-deprecating apology.

"You haven't changed, either," she said. And with that, the past evaporated. Andrea was not in love with him—never had been, she told herself. They finished breakfast as two old friends who found each other amusing.

"You can imagine how surprised I was when the name the museum gave me was yours." Clayton raised a hand just slightly above table level and the waiter arrived to refill their coffee cups. "I asked the curator at the Victoria and Albert Museum to recommend someone to authenticate and restore a bunch of old drawings that have come down through my wife's family. 'Andrea Perkins is the best in the field,' they said. 'Andrea Perkins?' I said, 'Yes,' they said. 'You mean Andrea Perkins with the red hair and centerfold body?' I said. 'That's the one,' they said. Then, to find out you were here—in London—working on a project for them . . ."

". . . which is almost finished."

"That's perfect. You can come stay with us in the country."

"No, I can't. I'm committed to another project as soon as I finish here."

"This is not just an invitation to be a houseguest. Deborah—my wife—wants to hire you." This was the first time Clayton had mentioned the name of his second wife. "She owns a gallery, which she inherited, here in London. One of her ancestors, a guy named Cecil Fetherston, founded the gallery. Maybe you know of him."

"I think so. A Victorian artist who did portraits and life-drawings, primarily."

"That's right. At least the drawings we have are *supposed* to be by him. Deborah wants to know for sure. They're not in great condition. There are a lot of brown spots on them. But if the pictures are authentic, and if they're worth it, she wants them restored."

"Probably foxing."

"What?"

"That's what the brown spots are."

"Okay. You see? You've diagnosed the problem already."

"I'm guessing. And anyway, knowing what's wrong and setting it right are not the same."

"The thing is, there are several people who are extraordinarily interested in buying them. I can't understand why. Pencil sketches, some pen-and-ink, and a few watercolor landscapes are about all that's there. They seem pretty pedestrian to me—although there's one rather erotic drawing of a nude couple that I like. Actually, the man is hardly more than a sketched-in outline except for one fully realized hand placed about mid-thigh on the lady. But she makes you look twice. She's got—what's the nineteenth-century equivalent of pizzazz? She's a little plump for my taste, but there's a really wicked, sexy smile on her sweet little face. You don't expect a Victorian woman to look so pleased with herself in such a compromising situation."

"Are the drawings signed?"

"Signed or initialed. The nude is locked away. It seems to be the best of the lot. But I brought another one with me. I'll show it to you before we leave."

"If they've been in the gallery for such a long time, why the sudden interest in restoring them?"

"It's because of Sybil, the manager of the gallery, really. After Deborah's father died, the man who had managed the gallery for God-knows-how-long decided to quit rather than take orders from a woman he remembered as a rather unpleasant little girl. On the recommendation of a friend of Deborah's—maybe more an acquaintance than a friend, but at any rate, a woman she knew who writes an art column for one of the newspapers and sometimes appears on television—we hired Sybil Forbes. Sybil—the new manager—came across the drawings when she was taking inventory. She happened to show them to the newspaper columnist, who mentioned them in her column, and we began to get inquiries. Strangely enough, two customers in particular are practically stepping on each other to buy them first. One is a writer who is doing a biography of William Gladstone. He apparently thinks that unpublished sketches from the Victorian era will add authenticity to his book. Actually, the only one he wanted to buy was of the nude charmer and her friend. He asked to borrow the rest to have them reproduced as illustrations. But if we refuse, I think he'd buy the lot. The other eager customer is an American collector with lots of bucks.''

"So why not just sell them?"

"We don't know what they're worth."

"In the art world, a picture is worth whatever anyone is willing to pay."

"But if they're really good, Deborah wants to keep them. That's why she wants an expert to take a look."

"It shouldn't be difficult to find a qualified person to examine them for you."

"Deborah won't settle for just anyone. She wants you. She always wants the best. That's why she married me."

"She must not have checked your references very closely."

"I think you'll like her," Clayton said. "She's nice." Then he added, "And rich."

"Nice and rich. That figures."

"She is both, really. I'm sure she'll pay you above the going rate for your expertise."

Andrea was annoyed with him again. "That's hardly the point. I have another assignment to go to. I have plane reservations to Los Angeles. People are expecting me." And though she was not going to discuss it with Clayton, the most important reason for going to California was that Aldo Balzani had said there was a good chance that an extradition matter might take him to California next, and he could meet her there.

"A few phone calls will take care of all that."

"No. I'm sorry."

"Of course, *you* know how much time would be involved in something like this—I don't," Clayton said in his most charming manner, "but I wouldn't think it would take long. Maybe a couple of days."

"It depends on a variety of things—the type of paper, where and how long the drawings have been stored...lots of things." Andrea took the napkin from her lap and laid it on the table beside her empty plate. "I have to be leaving. I told them at the V & A I'd be there by eleven."

Clayton reached for the manila envelope that had stood propped against his chair. "Take this with you," he said. "When you have a few minutes, take a look at it. See if it's worth restoring."

"Clayton—" she began, still planning to refuse.

"Just look at it." He stood, then went around and pulled her chair out for her. "If nothing else, it will give me an excuse to see you again."

In the lobby, Clayton kissed Andrea lightly on the cheek, then stepped back out of reach when she tried to return the envelope to him.

"I'll call you tomorrow," he said, then hurried away through a group of hotel guests waiting to board a sightseeing bus parked near the front door.

Andrea, instead, avoided the crowd and made her way toward the side exit. She had not agreed to examine the drawing, and yet there it was in her hand.

She stopped just outside the door under the awning to stash the manila envelope safely inside her canvas tote bag.

Ahead of her on the street, a police car drew up to the curb and retrieved two orange roadblock cones. Andrea suddenly remembered the accident and shivered as she hurried toward a taxi stand. There was no comfort in the thought that once the cones were taken away, there would be nothing to indicate anything out of the ordinary had happened that morning on Davies Street.

THREE

THOUGH THE DAY REMAINED gray and damp, a jogging suit—and even sunglasses—attracted little attention in Hyde Park. The only notice given the athletic-looking figure seated on a bench at the side of a footpath was an occasional nod from one of the similarly dressed exercise enthusiasts who ran or jogged past.

Mist so fine as to be almost invisible drifted and swirled and stuck to solid objects in beads of moisture. The drops of water collected on the bare branches of a nearby oak showered onto the hooded jacket and ran in rivulets down the jogger's tinted lenses each time the chilly wind moved through. The jogger, however, was too absorbed remembering the accident on Davies Street to notice the blurred view of the park.

It was an accident. No one planned for the taxi to hit her. Yet the fact remains that she could not be more dead if I had pushed her. That was something that was never discussed. Death was never mentioned, for God's sake. We never thought—I never thought—that someone would be lying in the middle of the street with her guts crushed under the wheels of a taxi. That was not part of the bargain. Get the Fetherston drawings and get away. That was it—that was all! We never discussed murder.

The jogger's jacket was uncomfortably wet on the inside, cold and clammy with sweat under the arms and in the center of the back.

It was an accident—not murder. A bloody, God-awful, absurd accident, which was all her own fault! She caused it! If she had just let go of the briefcase... She was accidentally killed. And she accidentally happened to be the wrong girl!

The sounds in the park were muted by the mist. The clopping of horses' hoofs could be heard nearby on Rotten Row, and beyond that, the drone of traffic in Kensington Road. The ordinariness of the sounds were soothing to the occupant of the bench who slumped against the backrest and tried to relax.

The wrong girl! How was I supposed to know? Get the envelope—that's what I was told to do. But which bloody envelope? At least a dozen landed on the floor in Claridge's. How was I to know which one?

It was easy to make such a mistake. The girl's hair was the right color and she was carrying a briefcase. And she's dead.

A duck from the long and winding lake—the Serpentine—waddled across the path. It pecked at a soggy crust of bread in the dead grass as though nothing had happened, as though this day was no different from any other.

The way she lay there on the street—her arms above her head and her legs spread apart... it was disgusting. Obscene. Someone should have pulled her skirt down. Just lying there—spread-eagled—in public—she looked as if she were willing to take on all comers.

A gray-haired man in a nylon parka jogged along the path in front of the bench. "Your muscles will tighten up if you sit there too long," he said with an appraising glance. His voice was breathy and labored but tinged with the disdain of one who has not yet given in to the pounding in his chest.

Until the blood soaked through the white slip that was bunched around the girl's waist...

"You've got to keep moving." The man waved and picked up speed, buoyed by his apparent superior endurance.

"Right. I'm just taking a breather."

It was strange how fast the crowd collected when they heard her scream. But no one noticed me. They were too shocked at seeing her lying in the street with her skirt above her waist.

A sudden eddy of mist caught a handful of decaying leaves and swirled them briefly above the ground, then dropped them again a few inches from where they had lain.

If I had pushed her, no one would have known. I could have committed murder in the middle of London in the middle of a crowd and no one would have suspected.

Though the fear of discovery had faded, the exhilaration had not. Laughter bubbled up and was choked back like vomit.

My God, murder! Is that what it's been about all along? Is that what's supposed to happen next?

The jogger bent to tie a shoelace, then began to run at a steady pace across the park past the Bathing Lido, the restaurant, the Serpentine Gallery, and across the intersection toward the Victoria and Albert Museum.

If stealing the drawings gets too complicated, then... murder may be the only way.

DESPITE THE forbidding appearance of the Victoria and Albert's massive stone exterior, the museum reminded Andrea of a gigantic lava lamp. It seemed to be continually bubbling with different colors and interesting shapes. There was nothing static there; indeed, it was in a constant state of change. Even the building itself had no single design. It was a combination of six different schemes begun by a builder in 1855, continued by two officers of the Royal Engineers, and more or less completed by an architect in 1909. The original name had not been permanent, either. Christened as the Museum of Manufactures, it moved on to the title of Museum of Ornamental Art, then—finally, one presumes—the Victoria and Albert.

Rooms had been added and others had been combined. Gardens had been planted and others uprooted. There had been continual plastering and painting and moving of walls. The interiors had been refurbished, then later disparaged. In the 1960s, it was thought that the background should fade to obscurity behind the displays and exhibits, and so the decor had been altered to a stark and colorless state. Recently, a new appreciation of Victoriana had emerged, and the original heavy ornamentation was being restored.

If the V & A were to be categorized at all, Andrea thought it could be done under the headings: *That Which Represents Victoria*, and *That Which Represents Albert*. In the Victoria column (under the subheadings Romantic and Artistic) would be listed the national collection of miniature paintings, classical sculpture, a vast collection of John Constable oil paintings, and displays of jewelry, netsuke, costumes, gold and silverwork. Representing Albert (subheaded Mechanical and Utilitarian), were such things as ironwork, clocks, furniture, woodwork, pottery, and porcelain, which was a toss-up—it could go in either category. A number of departments would still be left unclassified, including the one where Andrea was currently employed, the Fakes and Forgeries section.

Here, the museum boldly displayed its previous errors in judgment. The paintings, statuary, documents, and artifacts exhibited on the walls and in glass cases had been collected, originally, in good faith as genuine. Later, more sophisticated examination proved that they were not. Andrea admired the museum's audacity. After all, most museums had their share of fakes, but the V & A had the courage to admit to being duped and the humor to display the mistakes they had made. During her stay, she had identified an additional number of clever forgeries from the museum's vast collection. The newly identified fakes would be used on a rotating basis with the ones now on display.

This morning she entered the building from Exhibition Road. The lobby, as usual, was filled with visitors consulting guidebooks and each other as to which of the sections they should tackle first.

Andrea dodged the crowd and took the most direct route to her small office—through the Gothic art gallery. The room held no distractions for Andrea. Though Gothic art had taken on respectability over the centuries, the exhibits typified the earliest definition. During the Middle Ages, *Gothic* had been a derisive term, relating to the barbarian tribes of Goths who overran the Roman Empire and destroyed many of its previous artistic achievements. Displayed here were early Gothic imitations of classical Roman art.

The Spanish gallery, which she entered next, was another she could quickly pass through with no regrets. In fact, she always kept her eyes straight ahead so she would not have to look at an immense and particularly gruesome fifteenth-century tempera-and-gilt painting on wood of the Crucifixion.

On the other hand, she could never go through room 26—the last in her path to the office—without stopping. There, a statuette of the Madonna and Child always drew her attention. It was only eight and a half inches tall and carved from boxwood by the sixteenth-century German artist Veit Stoss. What made it so extraordinary were the expressions on the faces of the two small figures. Unlike the usual pose of the holy pair in which they gazed into each other's eyes in mutual admiration, this mother and child seemed to acknowledge the presence of the viewer. It was as though the proud mother with the peasant face was saying to the visitors with their cameras and their guidebooks, "Isn't this the most beautiful child you have ever seen?" And the ordinary—no, plain-looking—baby with the self-assured smile seemed content with the thought, "My mother says I'm beautiful, so it must be true."

This morning, Andrea had time for only a momentary pause, and soon continued toward the short flight of steps that led down to her office. As she glanced at her tote bag, switching it to the hand away from the stair railing, she was aware once again of the drawing that Clayton Foley had pressed upon her. He had not changed at all, she thought. He always managed to get what he wanted.

FOUR

NEAR CLOSING TIME that day, Henry March swung open the door to the museum's basement workroom and announced to Andrea that she had a visitor.

Henry was "given" to Andrea when she began her assignment at the Victoria and Albert. The young man had been hired by the museum because of his near-the-top standing in his graduating class from the Art History Studies program at the University of London. Though he had been at the V & A for more than a year, he had not yet secured a permanent position in any of its nine curatorial departments, for Henry March in the flesh was not nearly as agreeable as Henry March on paper. His fine academic record had secured him his position, but once on the scene, he managed to offend almost everyone with his undergraduate brashness. He had a total disregard for "that's the way it's always been done," and his preference for wearing jumble-sale clothing hadn't helped. To date, his responsibilities at the museum were mostly of the lifting and carrying type. He referred to himself as a floating dogsbody. Andrea thought of him as indispensable.

"She's waiting in your office."

"Who is it, Henry?"

"A la-di-da lady."

Andrea did not look up. She was brushing her special concoction of hot glue from the top of a double boiler onto a wooden frame. The frame would be used to stretch a neglected oil painting back into shape. The canvas, a recent donation to the V & A, had been stored for a number of years in the donor's damp basement. When it was rediscovered, it was thought to be a genuine Vermeer. However, Andrea had determined that it was not by the Dutch genius but was an excellent painting nonetheless, and worthy of a home in the Fakes and Forgeries section.

"Did the lady say what she wants?"

"I was not worthy to be told either her mission or her name. Her exact words were"—and with this, Henry affected a convincing falsetto—"'Tell Miss Perkins I am a contributor to the museum and wish to see her.'"

"I hope you were polite."

"I didn't curtsey, but I did offer her a chair."

Andrea attached a clamp to the corner of the frame, then placed the damaged canvas beside it, ready to be affixed when the glue was dry.

The painting was titled *A View of the City of Delft*. The style of the artist was marked by a pervading serenity and order. Reflected in the calm water of the canal and overhung with luminous clouds, the church spire, the quaint buildings, the fishing boats all seemed to exist in permanence and timelessness because of the artist's mastery of color and brushwork. The scene was typical of those chosen by Johannes Vermeer, whose signature appeared in the lower left corner—though the painting had actually been done by Han van Meegeren.

This was the fifth van Meegeren painting in the style of Vermeer that Andrea had been commissioned to restore, appraise, or denounce. She had developed a grudging admiration for the Dutch art faker whose treachery might never have been exposed had he not numbered Hermann Goering among his unsuspecting clients.

Van Meegeren was arrested after the war in connection with a sale to the Nazi field marshall. His defense against treason was his admission that he was a counterfeiter. "Would I cheat a Nazi of such high rank," he asked the court, "if I respected him? What greater insult could I inflict than to sell him a forgery. And further, can you imagine *my* fate if I had been discovered?"

The court still was not convinced. Because of the high quality of van Meegeren's work, his confession was not believed. As a last resort, he had his painting equipment delivered to the courtroom, whereupon he set up an easel with a blank canvas and demonstrated his extraordinary painting technique for the benefit of his astonished accusers.

Andrea took off her cotton smock and smoothed the collar of her silk blouse. Her usual work clothes were blue jeans and washable shirts, but she had not had time to change after her meeting with Clayton Foley at Claridge's.

Henry unabashedly appraised her. With a grin he repeated the advice that almost everyone in the museum—except Andrea—had given *him*, "You really should pay more attention to good grooming."

"What are you talking about?"

"That." He pointed to a white blob of glue just above the hem on the front of Andrea's dark gray skirt.

"Damn." Andrea flicked off the dried glue with her thumbnail, but a white circle still remained.

"Take it off, and I'll get that spot out in no time."

"Don't be an idiot."

"It was worth a try. I suppose I have the same sort of fascination you Americans have with the Scots and their kilts. I'd like to know what American girls wear under their skirts."

"You're a cheeky devil."

"And you're beginning to talk like a Brit." Henry leaned his back against the wall and slid down to a sitting position on the floor.

"Don't get comfortable." Andrea went to the worktable and the painting she had been repairing. "You can start cleaning this canvas."

"You mean I'm going to be entrusted with something other than a broom and a dustpan?"

"Shouldn't you be?"

"Of course." He obviously was pleased. "It's just that, as a general rule, my talent is left untapped."

"Well, tap away. I'll go see what the la-di-da lady wants."

Andrea's temporary office was a windowless cubbyhole at the top of the basement stairs. She had chosen it in preference to three larger spaces because of its proximity to the workroom. The furnishings consisted of a large nondescript wooden desk jammed against the wall and a stenographer's chair, which, because of the size of the desk, sat approximately in the center of the room. The only other furniture was an eighteenth-century ebonized beechwood dining chair. When purchased, it was thought to have come from Horace Walpole's great parlour at Strawberry Hill in Twickenham but later proved to be a clever copy. Uncomfortable as it was ornate, the chair had done nothing to improve the disposition of the woman who was sitting there waiting for Andrea.

"Ah. Miss Perkins?"

"Yes. You wanted to see me?"

"Indeed." The woman appeared to be in her early thirties and was a testimonial to London's finest fashion designers, cosmetologists, and hairdressers. She wore a white wool suit and a black wide-brimmed hat that was made of the same supple leather as her gloves and shoes. Her hair was blond and shoulder length. Her eyes were Wedgwood blue, as was the subtly applied eye shadow. A minuscule layer of oil-based makeup enhanced the classic English transparent look of her skin. Her lips, which might have seemed thin on a well-scrubbed face, appeared full and voluptuous, outlined in bright apricot and filled in with a more delicate peach shade. The overall effect was camera-ready. "I'm Deborah Foley," she said. "I understand you had breakfast this morning with my husband."

"Oh. Yes. Clayton and I were at Harvard together." Andrea heard herself almost stammering.

"So I understand."

The two women openly stared at each other with curiosity. After a moment, Andrea turned the stenographer's chair around and sat facing her guest. Leaning forward in what she hoped was a friendly attitude, she said, "I'm pleased to meet you, Mrs. Foley."

When Andrea glanced down, she caught sight of the circle of glue on her skirt directly on top of her knee. It suddenly seemed as big as a dinner plate. She quickly clamped her hand over the spot, but knew it was too late. Deborah Foley was the kind of woman who could spot a missing button or a wine stain from across a hotel lobby, and in Andrea's small office they were sitting practically knee to knee.

"It's Deborah. Please."

"Deborah, then. And I'm Andrea."

"Clayton told me how successful you are as an artist."

"I'm a technician, not an artist. I do restoration and authentication."

"But surely it takes just as much talent—perhaps a different kind—to restore a work of art as to create it."

Andrea started to protest, but Deborah Foley hurried on.

"You were recommended to us as the very best in your field. That's why we are so anxious for you to come to us in the country—to Rushwood House on the fifteenth. That, and because you and Clayton are such old friends, of course." Her smile parted the peach-tinted lips in a flash of extraordinarily white teeth. "He did invite you, didn't he?"

"Yes, but I'm sorry, I won't be able to come. My work here will be finished in a few days—"

"But you must!" The urgency, the actual alarm in Deborah Foley's voice, startled Andrea to silence. "Clayton showed you one of the Fetherston drawings, didn't he?"

"Yes—"

"Which one?"

"It was a rather stiffly posed gentleman with an impressive beard," Andrea said.

"Prince Albert. Or maybe Disraeli. What kind of beard? It doesn't matter. The point is, at least you got an idea of the condition of the drawings."

"I haven't had a chance to examine it closely, but it doesn't seem badly damaged. There's some discoloration—"

"Yes." Deborah nodded her agreement with the air of one expert to another. "Discoloration."

"Reddish brown fox marks often show up on old prints and drawings."

"Yes, the pox marks." Deborah hurried on, "Andrea, the Cecil Fetherston drawing you have is one of a dozen or so that have been in my family for generations. Cecil was the family black sheep who no one mentioned until recently. It seems he murdered some little prostitute and was hanged for his sins. But a few months ago, Malcolm Putney wrote an article about Fetherston. Did you happen to see it?"

"Not that I recall."

"It was in the *Times*, I think, and only mentioned Fetherston. The article actually was about William Gladstone. Gladstone was one of our prime ministers. A prime minister is rather like one of your presidents, I think. Gladstone served during Queen Victoria's reign."

"Yes. He was a real thorn in Victoria's side all four times he was elected." Andrea was not proud of herself for this irrelevant comment. It was about as subtle as saying, I know, I know. But she *did* know who William Gladstone was, and she did *not* care to be talked down to by Deborah Foley.

"At any rate," Deborah went on, unperturbed, "Malcolm Putney is writing a biography of Gladstone, and he mentioned Fetherston in the article. Ever since the wretched piece appeared, we've been hounded by people determined to buy the drawings."

"That doesn't sound like such a terrible problem."

"Not in itself—although we haven't decided whether we want to sell or not. At least I haven't." She paused long enough to brush a speck of plaster, which had fallen from the peeling ceiling, from the sleeve of her white suit.

"Is it a matter of having them appraised?" Andrea still could not understand how she fit into all this.

"That's part of it but not all. The drawings need to be restored and appraised, yes. But, most important, we have to establish ownership. Right now, if they were stolen, the thief could claim that they were discovered somewhere else. They need to be cataloged and documented by someone we trust. And Clayton trusts you." Deborah's voice softened suddenly, and there was a hint of wistfulness in her words. "He doesn't respect or trust many people."

Andrea looked up from the white spot on her skirt that had caught her attention again. For a fleeting instant, there was a look of vulnerability, even sadness, in Deborah's Wedgwood-blue eyes. Could it be that all was not well with the Clayton Foleys?

"The first step," Andrea said, "would be simply to photograph them all, and if nothing else, give copies to your lawyer."

"Yes. We've done that. Our solicitor has copies. But some of the drawings are in such abysmal condition that the signatures and even the features of some of the subjects are covered over with those brown spots. What did you call them?"

"Foxing."

"Yes, foxing. I'll remember that."

Her expression was like that of a child who is determined to memorize her address and telephone number. Against her will, Andrea began to feel sorry for the gorgeous Mrs. Clayton Foley, who seemed to have confidence only in her appearance.

"I suppose it's all right to tell you..." Deborah continued uncertainly, "did Clayton mention that there's been an attempt to steal them?"

"No, he didn't."

"After Putney's article, we moved the drawings to our country place from the gallery—I inherited the gallery where Cecil Fetherston did most of his work. Anyway, when we began to get inquiries about the drawings we took them with us to Rushwood House, mostly out of curiosity—just so we could see what all the hubbub was about. But the thief apparently didn't know this and broke into the gallery."

"Why do you think it was the Fetherston drawings he wanted?"

"The cabinet where they had been kept was broken into, and nothing was taken. The night watchman was struck from behind and got a nasty cut on the head." Then, in a tone that suggested it cost her a lot to ask a second time, she said, "You will help us, won't you?"

Andrea had no valid reason to refuse. It would be at least another ten days before Aldo could pry himself loose from the Florentine police department to meet her. If the damage to the drawings was as simple as Deborah Foley described, cleaning them would mean only a few extra days. "I suppose so," she said. "But I'll need some help. Is it all right if I bring my assistant?"

"Of course!" Deborah smiled. Standing to leave, she said, "Clayton will be so pleased."

"Yes. I imagine he will be," an amused voice said from the doorway. Neither woman had realized the man was there until he spoke. He was tall and slim and fair-skinned. A damp strand of blond hair fell across his forehead. His smile was boyish and mischievous. "And I'll be pleased too, for that matter."

"Arthur." Deborah sounded annoyed. "I thought you were going to meet me at the Cromwell Road entrance."

"And I thought you were going to be there fifteen minutes ago."

"Andrea, this is my impatient brother, Arthur Fetherston."

"Impatient, impoverished"—Arthur reached for Andrea's hand and kissed it—"and impressed."

"How do you do?" Andrea retrieved her hand and took a small step backward.

"Very well, on occasion," he said.

He could have been invented by Evelyn Waugh, Andrea thought. *Brideshead Revisited* instantly leapt to mind. Arthur Fetherston reminded her of the flawed but beautiful Lord Sebastian Flyte who made such a sensuous scene. The difference was, however, that Arthur Fetherston—to judge from his appraisal of Andrea—would have chosen a female companion instead of Charles Ryder.

"Good. It's settled then," Deborah said. "We'll expect you for the weekend."

"I'll stop by for you if you like," Arthur said.

"Thank you, but Henry, my assistant, has a van. I'll be carting along some equipment and it will be simpler if we drive down together."

With a shrug, Arthur turned and started toward the hall. Deborah followed, but paused in the doorway.

"Tomorrow," she said, "I'll send you a copy of the Malcolm Putney article and a list of the other guests who will be there." With a quick wave of the hand she left the office.

Other guests, Andrea repeated to herself. She already regretted agreeing to go. She had accepted an invitation for a working weekend, not a social outing. Never mind. She and Henry would restore the drawings and the others could socialize as much as they liked.

She still did not understand all the commotion about the Fetherston drawings. He was only one of several artists who had become financially successful because they had caught the attention of Queen Victoria. But certainly he could not be numbered with British giants like Constable and Gainsborough.

On the taxi ride between Claridge's and the Victoria and Albert Museum, Andrea had briefly inspected the drawing that Clayton Foley forced on her. The delicate pen-and-pencil sketch did not seem particularly impressive, skillful, but with very little hint of originality. Perhaps she had missed something.

She decided to examine the drawing a second time, and reached in her skirt pocket for the small key to her desk drawer.

To her surprise, which turned to a sense of foreboding, she realized, as she started to insert the key in the lock, that the drawer was open. The lock had been forced and the drawing was gone.

FIVE

ANDREA REACHED INTO her purse for Clayton Foley's business card and tried the first telephone number listed. There was no answer. She tried the second listing and Clayton picked up immediately.

"Foley here."

"Clayton? It's Andrea."

"What a nice surprise to be driving down M forty and hear your voice. Where are you?"

"In my office."

"Good. I'm just coming into Marylebone Road. I can be with you in fifteen minutes if you have something nefarious in mind."

"This is serious, Clayton."

"What could be more serious than something vile and wicked?"

It was hard to believe now that she had once thought him charming. "I met your wife this afternoon," she said.

"Yes, she told me she was going to drop by and have a look at you." There was resignation in Clayton's voice. Then he said something odd. "I hope she was coherent."

"She was very nice." Andrea did not stop to question his last remark. The loss of the Fetherston drawing was all that concerned her at the moment. "Deborah left only a few minutes ago. I tried to catch her, but she was already out of the building and rather than wait until she'd had time to get to your flat, I called you."

"What is it? What's the matter?"

"The drawing you gave me this morning is gone. It's been stolen."

There was the sound of an impatient car horn on the other end of the phone. Traffic hummed in the background, but for several seconds there was only silence from Clayton Foley.

"I brought the envelope back here and locked it in my desk drawer," Andrea hurried on. "Someone forced the lock while I was in the workroom this afternoon. I called the security office here at the museum, but I haven't called the police. I thought you or Deborah could give a better description."

"Andrea, I'm sorry I ever gave you that bloody drawing."

"I thought it would be perfectly safe in my desk."

"No. I mean, what if you'd been in the office alone when the thief broke in? It never occurred to me that I was putting you in any kind of danger."

All the same, Andrea thought, he might have warned her. At breakfast, he had neglected to mention that there had already been one attempted theft. "Deborah said the gallery had been broken into."

"The gallery? Oh. Well, yes, she and Sybil, our manager, thought it had something to do with the drawings. But I...*watch where you're going, you idiot!* Sorry. A furniture lorry almost ran me into the rail."

"Clayton, I'm going to hang up." She was suddenly angry at him. "Do you want me to call the police?"

"No. I'll do it. Honest, kiddo, I'm sorry to have gotten you mixed up in this. Just forget the whole thing."

Oh, sure. Now that she felt responsible for the damned drawing—now that it had been stolen from her desk—just forget it. "I told Deborah I'd see what I could do to restore the miserable drawings."

"I'll explain to her. No need for you to get involved."

"Oh, shut up. I'll see you this weekend."

Andrea hung up the phone and reached for her coat on a wall peg, took her canvas tote bag and umbrella from the desk drawer, locked her office and started down the quiet corridors of the V & A.

Closing time on weekdays was ten minutes before six. It was almost six-thirty now. Andrea's high heels rang on the tile floor as she entered the Fakes and Forgeries gallery. She liked having the long, narrow room all to herself. Only when the gallery was empty could the green-and-white mosaic floor be fully appreciated. The floor, like the exhibits in the glass cases on the walls, was another *opus criminale* (as it was dubbed by the first director of the museum). The myriad tiny tiles had been set in place by the nineteenth-century women inmates of Woking Prison.

The theme of the mosaic pattern was nautical and featured a tondo—a circular portrait—of a sleeping Neptune with his trident at rest beneath his chin. Circling the sea god's head were three vicious-looking fish. Andrea wondered if the female prisoners had strayed from the original design and turned the portrait into a protest or warning. She suspected that they had intentionally closed the eyes of Neptune, making him appear helpless and ineffectual, and curved the mouths of the captured fish downward to give them a predatory look. And why, she wondered, did Neptune, who looked placid, but nonetheless was in possession of the deadly trident, remind her of Deborah Foley's brother, Arthur Fetherston?

"G'night, Miss." The guard at the Exhibition Road exit touched the bill of his cap, then opened the front door as Andrea came through to the lobby. "It's still wet out there, I'm afraid."

"Yes, I thought it might be." She unsnapped the tab of her umbrella as she stepped out onto the rain-washed marble steps. "Good night." The door closed behind her.

The nighttime clouds had drifted down to sit upon the ground. As if painted with an overloaded brush the city lights were smeared and indistinct against this backdrop. The drizzle continued, but it was not heavy enough to bother with an umbrella, Andrea decided. She slipped her wrist through the leather thong and pushed her hand deep into her pocket. Sliding the straps of her bag over her shoulder, she bunched the lapels of her coat around her neck.

At the corner of Cromwell Road she hailed a taxi and gave the driver her Bloomsbury address.

Andrea was usually too busy to feel lonely. But tonight, sitting alone in the back of the cab with its fogged-over windows she had an almost desperate need to have someone she cared about beside her. She wanted to be with someone she could talk to about the missing drawing. She wanted to complain to someone about Clayton Foley, and amuse them with her version of the knee-to-knee conversation with Deborah Foley in the tiny office at the V & A, and describe how Arthur Fetherston had suddenly materialized in the doorway like a sullen and sexy apparition. If only *Aldo* would materialize right now.

At times, Andrea felt more like a stranger in England than she had in Italy, even though her college-brand Italian sometimes caused problems and she found the lira more difficult to deal with than the British pound. But she felt at home anywhere with Aldo.

As the taxi turned onto Woburn Place a few blocks from her hotel, Andrea gazed through the misted window at the nighttime lights of the small businesses crowding each other along the street. There was a pizza parlor, an Indian take-out restaurant, a small market whose proprietor was busily moving crates of fresh fruits and vegetables from the sidewalk bins to the narrow aisle inside the store before closing time.

Andrea's spirits rose several degrees when she noticed a small revival movie theater at the end of the block. The marquee read: *A Man Called Sledge*, a western starring James Garner.

"Stop at the corner," Andrea instructed the cabbie, "I can walk from here." She paid the fare and stood back as the taxi rounded the corner. When the streetlight changed, she crossed the street to the theater.

A young woman with two pink plastic clips in her frizzy hair sat in the ticket booth intent on something she was knitting with variegated orange yarn. "The feature's been running for fifteen minutes," she told Andrea without bothering to look up.

"I don't mind." She had seen the movie five times before.

With a shrug that said there was no accounting for the taste of weirdos who liked old movies, the ticket seller reluctantly dropped her knitting in her lap and sold Andrea a ticket.

Fewer than twenty people were sitting in the theater. Andrea felt her way to the center of a row halfway down the aisle. With the comfortable feeling the familiar can generate, she settled low in the seat and propped her feet on the back of the empty seat in front of her, smiling up at the rakish image of James Garner.

Andrea was not only a western movie fan, but with no conscious effort, she had become a minor authority. Westerns predated blue jeans and Kentucky Fried Chicken as favorite American exports the world over. No matter where her work took her, there was usually a movie house where John Wayne, James Garner, Gary Cooper, or one of the other American cowboy heroes filled the screen with dust as they galloped across the plains. It did not matter that the dialogue was dubbed in or subtitled in incomprehensible foreign phrases. With no sound at all the stories would still have been easy to follow.

Westerns were not only a reminder of home for Andrea, they were like giant family albums in which her Uncle Bob often starred, or more accurately, appeared. For years, her father's older brother had managed to support himself and a series of wives as a bit player in Hollywood.

As a child, Andrea had doted on her Uncle Bob because of his warmth and wit and the hilarious stories he told about his misadventures as an actor.

On the screen, James Garner had just finished a spectacular gunfight after his partner was shot in the back in a poker game. Andrea giggled to herself as she remembered the scene that would come next. Garner was going to organize a gang to steal a gold shipment. The gang included Claude Akins and—oh, God—there was Uncle Bob in an absurd mustache, his hair slicked down with what must have been cooking oil.

Near the end of the movie, after the robbery, there was another poker game sequence. This time, Garner played the members of the gang. Naturally, he won everyone else's share of the gold, which did not set well with Akins, Uncle Bob and company.

There! There was Uncle Bob's one close-up! Andrea grinned. Wow, he looked mean! Now. Stand up and kick the chair back from the table!

As Garner shot the partners one by one, Andrea remembered Uncle Bob's story about the uncooperative red dye capsule that refused to burst and spread like blood across his chest when he was shot. In order to save the scene, he had had to twist away from the camera and fall face down. He hit the ground with such force that it ripped off his mustache. Fortunately, his face was hidden by his hat, but the mustache lay there beside him like a giant cockroach.

Andrea was laughing when the lights came up, and the other members of the audience looked at her strangely as they all filed out into the lobby. But she felt restored.

It was not until she got back outside on Woburn Place where the chilling drizzle was now augmented by fog that she thought again of the dismal prospect of spending a weekend with Clayton and Deborah Foley in the Cotswolds.

THE NEXT DAY, as promised, Andrea received from Deborah Foley a messenger-delivered list of the guests who had been invited to the exhibit of the Fetherston drawings at Rushwood House.

The note was handwritten in a childish scrawl on expensive paper.

"Dear Andrea," it read, "Most of these people have a special interest in Fetherston the man or Fetherston the artist, and some of them seem determined to purchase all or some of the sketches.

"As I have no idea of the amount of time or effort involved in removing the 'foxing' (you see—I *did* remember!), we decided it was best to display the drawings 'as is' and then let you and your assistant (you *did* say you were bringing someone else, didn't you?) set to work on them.

"I am truly looking forward to knowing you better, Andrea. Regards, Deborah."

The guest list read:

"Malcolm Putney—he's the writer I mentioned who is at work on an autobiography of Gladstone. I *think* he calls it an autobiography, but I don't see how that's possible. Everyone has to write their own, don't they? I probably got it wrong, and I can't seem to find that article from the *Times*.

"Sybil Forbes—she's the manager of the Fetherston Art Gallery. She's good at taking care of the books, but I really question her taste in art sometimes. Maybe not in art—because I'm no expert—but certainly in clothes. I think you can tell a lot about people by the way they dress, don't you? Her wardrobe seems to run to pleated skirts, twin-sweater sets, and single strands of pearls.

"Lord and Lady Smith-Hamilton—they're American. People don't say 'nouveau riche' anymore, do they? That's probably unkind, at any rate. Mrs., my mistake, *Lady* Smith-Hamilton is the owner of a chain of dress shops that have a clever name which I can't for the moment, recall. And she *does* deserve the title. I understand she *paid* enough for it at an auction. Can you imagine?

"India Hamilton—the Smith-Hamilton's daughter, is a student at Oxford, I believe. She chooses to use only one of the surnames.

"Mandy Carruthers—she's a television person... talks about art and books on—I can't remember the name of her program. Oh, yes, 'The Art Beat of London.' Rather 'too cute,' wouldn't you say? Now this is a woman who knows about clothes! She must spend her entire salary at Harrods.

"I think Clayton and Arthur may have invited some other people. And of course they'll both be there."

Though Deborah Foley had written that the Malcolm Putney article was lost, the carelessly clipped column was folded inside her note.

"Here it is," she had written in the narrow margin, "I found it tucked beneath my desk blotter. I knew I'd put it *somewhere*. And no matter what the egotistical ass says—and in print, if you please—I have *not* given him permission to use the Fetherston drawings in his book."

Andrea unfolded the enclosed clipping and discovered it was not from the *Times*, but from a quarterly magazine titled *British Books and Authors*. Putney's article was on a page given over to a different guest columnist in each edition.

BIOGRAPHY, AUTOBIOGRAPHY AND/OR HISTORY?
By Malcolm Putney

In approximately the same amount of time that it would take you to butter and eat a scone, I will tell you, dear reader, how I turned musty history into steamy prose.

You can be sure that the title of my new book will be repeated later in this article, but you may as well get a pencil and write it down now: "The Autobiography of William Ewart Gladstone." Wait! Before you go scurrying away, hang on to my promise of *steamy prose* while I explain about musty history.

Ralph Waldo Emerson stated that "there is properly no history; only biography." Let's think about that for a moment, shall we? Hmmm. Now then, consider this quote from the noted historian Barbara Tuchman. She said, in summary, "The historian's task is to find out what really happened. We can never be certain that we have recaptured [history] as it really was. But the least we can do is to stay within the evidence." (I apologize for using two Americans as authorities, but as a breed, they do seem fascinated with history—possibly because they have so little of it of their own).

Squirrel away in your memory, or better still, if you are still holding on to that pencil, write down one word from Mr. Emerson—biography—and one word from Ms. Tuchman—evidence.

If you accept Emerson's premise that all we know of the past is what is written about men by other men to be read by still other men—biography—you can see how watered-down the events become in the telling. Why not, say I, eliminate the middleman and let the subject tell us of his own life?

Unfortunately, the previously mentioned William Gladstone has not been with us in earthly guise since 1898. What a pity the father of British liberalism can't describe in his own words what it was like being Prime Minister to a proletariat that called him "the people's William," and at the same time serving a Queen who referred to him as "a dreadful old man." And why, exactly, did Queen Victoria hate his guts? (The answer to this is perhaps the juiciest part of my book. Don't miss it!)

And think what he could tell us of Victorian London after dark. Few inhabitants knew the seamier side of the city as well as he. What compelled him to stroll the fetid streets that teemed with prostitutes who would frolic with their customers for the price of a glass of gin? How did a man like Gladstone sublimate his inordinate sexual drive and still keep his Calvinist conscience intact?

Oh, William. Why didn't you write it all down? Why didn't you leave your own life story behind instead of those gloomy books on theology that have done nothing but gather dust on the shelves of the Reading Room in the British Museum? Well, he didn't. And as he did not see fit to write his *own* autobiography—I've done it for him.

Ah, dear reader, you say that one cannot write another person's autobiography; that *bi*ography was the word I asked you to write down. But let us not quibble over semantics. Once you've read my book, you'll be convinced that it was set down by Gladstone himself.

And now to Ms. Tuchman's key word—evidence.

For the past two years I have been up to my handsome (if I do say so myself) Harold Macmillan mustache in *evidence*. I have sifted through and categorized nineteenth-century letters, records, documents, and—most interesting of all—the previously unpublished notebook of a Bow Street police captain (see chapter fourteen of my book for details).

But the *coup de maître* of the book is the collection of illustrations. I have arranged to include a series of recently uncovered, never-before-published drawings by Cecil Fetherston. Fetherston, a popular artist of the day, was an acquaintance of our hero and art tutor to Queen Victoria. One of the drawings in particular—which I have dubbed "The Balmoral Nude"—will titillate, and perhaps even shock you.

But I dare not say more. My purpose here is merely to whet your appetite for nineteenth-century gossip.

My publishers, Harrow and Sons, Limited, are committed to a release date six months hence. It is not too early, however, for you booksellers out there to order huge quantities of this rather large tome which, because of the superb quality of the writing, bears a higher than usual *art book* price.

You readers must cooperate as well. As soon as it is available, you must purchase one copy of *The Autobiography of William Ewart Gladstone* by Malcolm Putney for your own coffee table, and one for that of a friend.

I've done my part—and quite magnificently—by writing the book. So, you see, faithful followers, the rest is up to you.

Andrea laughed out loud when she finished reading Putney's article. She could not decide whether he was a super salesman or—as Deborah Foley described him—an egotistical ass.

As she folded the clipping, she noticed that Deborah had made another hasty notation on the back. "Putney's wife will also be at Rushwood. She teaches something or other at the University of London. Or maybe she won't be. He wasn't sure."

Andrea returned the clipping and note to the envelope and stuffed them into the pocket of her jeans. Then she locked her office and started toward the basement of the V & A. Through a small window in the stairwell she caught a glimpse of the swirling drizzle and the gray sky outside and, by contrast, found the artificial light of her workroom inviting as she settled down to check the canvas in front of her.

Across the city, the back booth of the Hammersmith Gardens Grill would have been in almost total darkness without the stubby candle on the table, even though it was only a little past noon.

"I've been waiting thirty minutes for you," he said when the woman slipped into the booth beside him.

"I couldn't find a taxi, and it takes a while on the tube." The flame of the candle wavered inside its red glass chimney and cast pale light on the man's empty coffee mug, the grease-spotted menu, a black plastic salt shaker, and a sticky bottle of Worchestershire sauce. The woman looked with distaste at the grimy restaurant. "Why did you pick this place to meet?"

"Do you know anyone who lives in Hammersmith?"

"No." She pushed the hood of her raincoat back and shook her hair free.

"Neither do I. That's why."

"I had hoped you'd come by my place last night. I wanted to see you." Searching his face, she saw the eagerness she had expected. But she knew that, at the moment, it was not for her. With resignation, she opened the shopping bag she had brought and handed him the manila envelope to make sure the Fetherston drawing was inside. It was not until he actually touched the heavy vellum that he began to relax. Then, turning to her, he said, "I've wanted to see you, too. I couldn't imagine why you were so late, getting here."

Without answering, she leaned her head back against the wooden booth and closed her eyes. She was tired. She felt drained.

The man glanced around the small dark restaurant. No one was watching them. The few other people there were seated at the bar absorbed in a rerun of a billiards competition on television.

"What could be keeping her, I thought." He leaned forward and kissed her neck just beneath her chin. "I decided that after your performance yesterday you must have taken up physical fitness more seriously than I suspected." She did not move. Her eyes were still closed. He undid the top button of her coat and traced the hollow at the base of her throat with the tip of his tongue. With his lips still against her skin, he said, "I thought you might have decided to jog all the way here."

Her laugh was more of sensual pleasure than of mirth. Her sudden surge of passion surprised her, as it always did. The unexpected always excited her the most—as when, in a crowded room, his hand brushed across her breast as though by accident. He was a genius of timing, she thought. Usually, it was at a cocktail party or an art exhibit. She would be deep in conversation—often with a stranger—and would have no idea he was anywhere nearby. Suddenly, she would feel his breath on her neck, or his hand slide across her hips, or his fingers lift her hair and his tongue touch her ear; quickly, deftly, so that no one else noticed. And then he would be gone, and she would be left—her legs trembling, her eyes crazy—talking gibberish to some unsuspecting soul.

Once, at a dinner party at the Savoy, when he was seated next to her, he had thrust his hand between her crossed legs. Beneath the tablecloth his fingers had crumpled the printed-silk of her evening dress and dug into the soft skin of her inner thighs. She had bitten her lip to keep from crying out—not from pain, though later there were yellow and blue bruises on both her legs, but from wanting him. Even though he and she had spent an unscheduled hour together in bed that morning, and even though he had promised to spend all the next night with her—still, if he had asked, she would have made love to him at that very moment. She would have pushed back her chair, left her napkin beside her wine glass and crawled under the table with him. For the rest of the evening, all she could think of was the two of them nude and coupling on the carpeted floor of the Savoy dining room amid the hand-sewn shoes and the hems of the Knightsbridge dresses.

Logic told her—when she bothered with logic—that it was the danger, the impossibility of the situation that made it so exciting.

There had been something of the same feeling the previous afternoon when she sat on the bench in Hyde Park and thought of the accident on Davies Street.

After it was over, after she realized that the girl had fallen in front of the taxi and been killed, and after the fear and revulsion had stopped pounding in her head, she had felt exhilarated.

Someone could have seen the accident. But no one had.

Someone could have told the police that she pushed the girl. Although she had not.

Someone she knew could have walked or driven by and recognized her at the moment she grabbed the girl's briefcase. But it had not happened.

She had been at the edge of discovery, the peak of danger, and had come away unscathed.

No one but the man beside her knew that she had been anywhere near Claridge's that morning—no one but the man whose hand beneath the table was moving slowly up her thigh.

"Let's go," she said and stood quickly.

"I suppose we must," he said, surprised at the suddenness with which she grabbed his hand. "I should be getting back."

"No. Not yet. Let's go to my flat."

She was halfway to the door before he had time to search his pockets for money to pay for his coffee.

SIX

THE DAY THEY were to leave for Rushwood House, Andrea and Henry March met in the basement workroom of the V & A to check the list of chemicals and equipment they would need to restore the Fetherston drawings. Henry sat atop a high metal stool—pencil and weathered pocket notebook in hand—and wrote down the items as Andrea called them off.

"Five ounces of calcium oxychloride," Henry repeated, then paused to scratch the side of his nose with the eraser end of the pencil.

"Better make that ten," Andrea said, "I doubt that we can depend on the local pharmacy for a refill if we don't have enough. Twelve ounces of hydrochloric acid, a bottle of hydrogen peroxide, two—no, make that three—five-gallon bottles of distilled water. I see that you have already packed the absolute alcohol and the ether. I'll bring my own brushes and miscellaneous equipment and...you're sure your photographer friend will let us borrow his flat baths?"

"They're in the van."

"And they're porcelain?"

"They're porcelain."

"A roll of blotting paper?"

"In the van."

"Two sheets of plate glass?"

"In the van."

"A plaster of Paris slab?"

"Got it. And a long-handled mallet."

"What's the mallet for?"

"I thought I'd try my hand at polo while we're there," Henry said, unwinding himself from the metal stool and tucking his faded T-shirt into his beltless jeans.

"I don't think they play polo in high-top tennis shoes."

"Then bugger it."

"I know it's a lot to ask, but bring along a jacket and a tie. We'll be having dinner with the gentry."

"Jacket and tie," Henry wrote in his notebook. Then, in alarm, he said, "Bloody hell! Do you suppose they'll expect me to wear pants and a shirt, too?"

"And shoes," Andrea said. "You do have some other shoes, don't you?"

"I have some Roman sandals, but considering the possibility of snow..."

"They'll be fine with a pair of sweatsocks."

"You Americans have no sense of style," Henry said from the doorway. "Even *I* wouldn't wear white socks after five o'clock."

MOTORWAYS, FREEWAYS, autostradas, autobahns—they are all the same, Andrea thought. Even if the local scenery had not been obscured by raw gashes cut through hillsides so that the concrete could be laid straight and flat, and even without the ugly guardrails that blocks the view on each side, there was no time to look anywhere but straight ahead or in the reflecting and rearview mirrors. Driving them was always a matter of skill versus nerve and size versus speed—especially in Great Britain where they insisted on driving on the wrong side.

Andrea was able to adjust fairly quickly to the British idiosyncrasy when she was at the wheel, but she found being a passenger frightening.

Each time an automobile or a lorry passed them Andrea had the feeling that the whole left side of Henry's battered VW van—and she along with it—was going to be scraped away and mangled.

"You can't operate the brake from over there," Henry said the fifth time Andrea slammed her foot against the floorboard.

"I'm sorry. It's having those chemicals jostling around in the back that's making me nervous," she said. "You're sure there's no danger of their banging into each other?"

Henry nodded but gave her no answer. He had already assured her, and she had seen for herself that they were carefully packed.

The ether concerned her the most. Later she would think how pointless it had been to worry about it in the car. It was perfectly safe surrounded by sheets of plastic bubble pack in a cardboard box in the back of the van. It was only after the bottle was unpacked and set out in plain view that it became dangerous.

To Andrea's relief, Henry slowed the van as they left the motorway just short of Oxford. The metal guardrails began to taper off, as did the number of traffic lanes. They drove through Witney and Burford and at last were on a narrow unpaved road. There was nothing now to obstruct the view of the countryside but occasional dry stone walls, which, Andrea thought, were things of beauty in themselves.

The drizzling rain had been left behind, along with the traffic. Pale sunlight slanted through barren trees with the deceptive look of warmth. As the van topped a low hill, the small village of Chipping Codsbury came into view on the downward-side of the rise. Clustered near an old woolen mill were a dozen or more early seventeenth-century stone cottages. They sat close together along a curving lane and were almost identical in design: all had two stories and slate roofs; most had two chimneys and gabled windows. All were built of the same buff-colored Cotswold stone and seemed to have risen as a unit from the dark, rich earth. The scene was so picturesque that Andrea asked Henry to pull over and stop for a moment.

Though it was still only midafternoon, the winter daylight would soon be gone. In the waning minutes, the sun seemed determined to dazzle the eye and quicken the heart.

"Over there," Henry said excitedly, "look!" He pointed beyond the village toward a field rising gently toward the horizon. On the left, breaking the line between earth and sky were bare-branched oak trees. At the edge of the copse was the blurred outline of an animal—head down—searching the ground.

"What is it? I can't quite make it out."

"Wait." Henry ran to the van and in a moment returned with a pair of binoculars.

Just as Andrea finished adjusting the lenses, the object of attention, a fallow deer, sauntered into a patch of full sunlight and turned its face toward her, as though it were posing. Andrea was speechless at the beauty of the moment. But even before the deer turned and merged once again with the shadows, Henry broke the spell.

Embarrassed at having taken part in a scene he pretended to consider maudlin, he asked, "Did you ever eat venison? If you're hungry, there's a pub down the road that features venison steaks. Their specialty is a sandwich the locals call a Bambi-burger."

Andrea knew he was being deliberately crude. Nevertheless, she could not forgive him immediately. She climbed back into the van without a word.

Minutes later, the sun was gone and the countryside was reduced to tones of gray. They drove on in silence for several miles.

Still holding the binoculars, Andrea reached down between the seats, found their empty case, and returned them. "Do you always carry these with you?"

"Usually."

"Why?"

"Promise you won't tell."

"Who would I tell?"

"You can't tell *anyone*. You can't tell the queen, you can't tell the BBC, and especially, you can't tell Prince Charles."

"Okay. I promise." Andrea was smiling again in spite of herself.

"I was issued those binoculars when I got my certificate as a spy."

"Oh, I see. And you've been spying on Prince Charles?"

"No. But you know how he goes on about preserving British architecture?"

"I've always admired that about him."

"Even so, you must never tell him that I sold the floor plan of the V & A to the Russians. You're shocked, aren't you? The Kremlin now knows where the gift shop is—the shortest route to the rest rooms—they even know not to order the shepherd's pie in the restaurant on Thursday."

"Henry March, they gave you the wrong certificate." Andrea laughed. "You're a certified nut."

Soon, the van crossed the bridge on the Rushwood River and turned up a long drive that led to the Foleys' country home, Rushwood House. A tranquil moment—and the last one for Andrea while she was in the Cotswolds.

Suddenly Henry jammed on the brakes with such force that the van skidded sideways on the narrow road before coming to a stop.

"Bloody stupid bitch!"

"Who? What—what happened?" Andrea had seen nothing.

"Look at her go! Just like we bloody weren't here!" Henry pointed through the front window at the rear end of a white Volvo as it took the next curve and disappeared from sight. "She came ripping out of that side road directly in front of us."

"At least we know your brakes are in good condition," Andrea said, catching her breath.

"She looked right at me as she pulled in front, just daring me to hit her."

"Well, thank heaven you didn't."

Henry backed the van, then headed it in the original direction. "Probably one of your fellow bloody guests for the weekend."

"I wouldn't know. I didn't see her. If she *is* a guest I wouldn't have recognized her anyway. I don't know any of the people who are going to be there except Deborah and Clayton, and Deborah's brother, Arthur."

Around the curve was a small signpost that said RUSHWOOD.

The van veered on to a narrow gravel drive that stretched like a darkened tunnel through barren beechwoods. Henry turned on the headlights. It was not yet late afternoon, but already the lengthy twilight of the English winter had set in—a sort of ten-watt compensation to daytime until night could make an entrance at a respectable hour.

"There she is again." Henry pointed ahead toward the distant white Volvo that sat idling between tall stone walls.

As the van drew closer, Andrea could make out a female figure in a fur hat and a shaggy fur coat as she left the car to open a heavy wrought iron gate. When the gate swung open, the woman jumped back into the Volvo, drove through, then quickly got out again to close the gate behind her.

By the time Henry's van reached the gate, all that was visible of the Volvo was the fading red glow of taillights.

SEVEN

THE SERIES of tragic events that ended with Cecil Fetherston, the Victorian artist, being hanged for murdering his mistress began soon after he purchased Rushwood House.

The original Rushwood House dated from the sixteenth century. It was built by the most prosperous of the local wool merchants as his manor house. The construction used the same Cotswold stone as the cottages in Chipping Codsbury, but there the similarity ended. Where the smaller homes were compact and cozy, the country house sprawled and towered.

By the end of the seventeenth century, early Jacobean influences still remained but the house had later undergone expansion and Georgian revisions. In the mid eighteen hundreds, when it was purchased by Cecil Fetherston, the house boasted—in addition to the drawing room, morning room, ante-room, dining room, great hall, and library—twenty-one bedrooms and three baths.

Fetherston's success had never been greater. His gallery was thriving and his own paintings and sketches were in demand. His popularity was due, in part, to the common knowledge that his work was favored by Queen Victoria, who engaged him as her personal art tutor.

Fetherston settled his wife and young son in the new home in the Cotswolds, though he was seldom able to join them there. The pressure of business kept him at the gallery in London, or, when summoned, in the company of the queen at Windsor Castle, at Osborne House in the Isle of Wight, or at Balmoral in Scotland.

Initially, he had been instructor to both Queen Victoria and Albert, the prince consort. Victoria's sketches were somewhat impressionistic, while Albert had, by far, the better grasp of the theory of drawing. His pleasure came from calculating the parallel and oblique perspectives of an object in relation to the ground line.

On one occasion at Balmoral, Fetherston and his two royal students trekked to a clearing on Craigendarroch Hill where they had an unobstructed view of the Ballater Railway Station. At the end of the session, Albert had what amounted to a diagram of the building that was accurate down to the number of panes in each window and bricks in the chimneys. Victoria's drawing of the building was much less detailed, and much more pleasing. It sparked the viewer's imagination and left him wondering about the unseen people inside the station and the destination of the train that was sure to arrive any second.

After Albert's illness and untimely death at the age of forty-two, drawing and painting in watercolors seemed to be the only diversions that could coax the queen from her obsessive mourning. When Fetherston's wife objected to his frequent sojourns away from home, he countered with the argument that though he would much prefer to be with his family, he could not in good conscience consider his own desires first when it was within his power to lighten the grief of the queen.

Because of the artist's privileged position in the royal household, he was granted access to the queen's private art collection. To his surprise, he saw reflected a royal delight in the nude form, both male and female. Among the prized statuary were John Bell's erotically posed *Andromeda*, William Geefs's half-nude *Paul and Virginie*, and William Theed's totally nude *Narcissus*.

Fetherston was particularly astonished by a larger-than-life-size painting by Anton von Gegenbaur titled *Hercules and Omphale*. It hung in Victoria's private apartment. Omphale, the queen of Lydia, was depicted wearing only a head scarf and a sensual smile while seated on the bare knee of Hercules, whom—according to Greek mythology—she kept for a time as her slave.

The revelation of Queen Victoria's taste in art prompted Fetherston to improve his own skills in life drawing. And this, in turn, led to his association—his obsession—with Emma.

Emma was introduced to him by the chancellor of the exchequer, William Gladstone. Fetherston had met the honorable gentleman more than once when they both had business with the queen.

Gladstone often roamed the nighttime streets of London, spreading the Gospel by word of mouth and through the religious tracts he handed to anyone who would accept them. His particular interest was in saving the souls of the many prostitutes who walked the streets and frequented the gin shops. One such girl was Emma.

Initially, it was an ideal arrangement for both artist and model. Emma found that reclining on a couch in the nude or standing on a marble pedestal was—if at times a bit dull and drafty—all in all, the easiest work she had ever done without her clothes on. For Fetherston's part, he was confident that he could view the girl objectively and enhance his skills in drawing the human body.

Until that point in his career, except for stiffly posed portraits commissioned by wealthy clients, Fetherston had concentrated on landscapes and still lifes. His mastery of inanimate objects falsely convinced him that the only challenge in painting from life would be perfecting the proper skin tone. Mixing paint that was either too pink or too pale had been the downfall of many an artist. Beyond that, using Emma as a model was no different from painting an abandoned boat beside the Thames, a field of cowslips, or a rosy Devonshire apple.

However, unlike still life objects, Emma moved. At first, this was merely annoying. Then, as the artist studied her closely, he detected a wantonness in her slightest movement. In repose, she would caress her knee, rub her cheek against her bare shoulder, chew and suck on her fingers. This discovery disturbed Fetherston so that his hands began to tremble, his breathing became unaccountably shallow, and his face appeared constantly flushed.

Even when Emma tried to be still, as he instructed, something about her would be in motion. A wisp of hair would escape from a hairpin and fall across her forehead. A hand would reach to rub an ankle. Lips would part, and a tongue would dart out to moisten them. But most amazing of all, when the room grew chilly, the tiny blue veins in her breasts seemed more pronounced and the nipples would stand erect and deep red.

With the exception of classes in life drawing and anatomy—in which he had been only one in a room full of students—Fetherston had seldom seen even his wife completely nude. Victorian convention conceded that a certain degree of nudity was necessary for copulation, and copulation was necessary to beget children. And that was that.

But to Emma, being without clothes was of no more consequence than if she *had* been an apple. And when Fetherston could resist temptation no longer and suggested he recline with her on the couch, she agreed without hesitation—for a slight adjustment in her fee.

Emma's unembarrassed lovemaking was a revelation to the artist, as was his own latent sexuality. And, he found, this newly discovered passion was not confined to the flesh but seeped into every aspect of his life. Colors were brighter. Music made him giddy with emotion. Literature quite often moved him to tears. The smell of the earth or the quiet beauty of early snow would send his soul soaring.

Unfortunately, it was not possible to share this new awareness of life with his wife in the Cotswolds. How could he, when the pressure of business kept him at his London gallery or in consultation with Queen Victoria?

He did, however, feel that he may have imparted something of his sensitivity to the queen. Her skill and perception as an artist improved with every sketch. It was almost as though she had experienced an awakening similar to the one Emma had inspired in him.

Of course Fetherston realized how absurd that thought was. The forty-four-year-old queen was in mourning. And though it had been two years since the death of Prince Albert, she was never seen in anything other than widow's black. Even her finest feature, her lustrous brown hair, was covered with a black cap and veil. Her small mouth never smiled. But, occasionally, Fetherston glimpsed a new animation in her eyes.

The world sympathized with her grief at the loss of her beloved Albert. No one begrudged her the reclusive life she sought—with the exception of a few men of government, including Gladstone. She lived with her memories, surrounded by her children, attended by a small retinue and protected by her indispensable servant and factotum, John Brown.

John Brown had come into the queen's service during one of her stays at Balmoral in Scotland. Now, it seemed, he attended her wherever she went. He had become the buffer encountered by anyone seeking access to the queen. Victoria, in a letter to her uncle Leopold, explained her dependence on the rugged thirty-nine-year-old Scotsman. She had, she wrote, "appointed that excellent Highland servant of mine to attend me always and everywhere...whether riding or driving or on foot; and it is a real comfort, for he is devoted to me—so simple, so intelligent, so unlike an ordinary servant, and so cheerful and attentive..."

Victoria's enthusiasm for John Brown was not shared by her family. Nor was it appreciated by officials of the government, particularly Gladstone. To the men who ran the country, it was bad enough to have to travel outside London to meet with the queen, when she did reluctantly agree to see them. And once at Windsor or Balmoral or Osborne, it was worse to be treated rudely by the disrespectful servant who seemed to have the run of the castle.

A great deal could be forgiven a grieving widow. However, when her mourning stretched beyond even Victorian acceptance into decades, the entire nation shared the sentiments of—by then—Prime Minister Gladstone. Eventually, the people resented the absenteeism of the queen. But in 1863, when Cecil Fetherston believed that it was his tutelage that assuaged her grief and was the reason for her heightened sensitivity, her bereavement was only two years old.

Grief of a different kind was to enter Fetherston's own life. It was sudden and devastating, and it culminated in violence and death.

The tragedy engulfed him one evening when he returned early from a trip to Windsor Castle and went straight from the train to meet his adored Emma. Running up the outside steps to her room above the gin shop, he paused on the landing to catch his breath, then flung open the door. A candle on a small table sputtered and flared in the sudden rush of air and enlarged to giant size the shadows on the wall of the two moving figures on the bed. Emma and her client were so actively engaged in what the man had paid for that they neither saw nor heard Fetherston enter.

The artist knew Emma was a girl of the streets when he hired her, and he had no reason to believe that she had changed. But it was not clear thinking that Emma had unleashed in him. And suddenly seeing her with another man, he was consumed with jealousy—followed quickly by hatred and murderous strength.

Fetherston's hand went to the knife he carried at his waist for scraping paint from old canvases. If the handle had been of lesser substance than steel it would have been crushed in his grip. Raising the blade high above his head, he struck at the heaving back of the man on top of Emma's wanton body.

But the man moved.

With a grunt like a rutting animal and a final jerking spasm, he rolled to one side. The knife grazed his neck and shoulder and struck Emma instead.

The blade pierced her flesh and bone and heart. The handle stood upright in the blue-veined breast next to the deep red nipple.

Emma's customer escaped into the night with superficial wounds. But Emma died. And there was a witness to the crime: William Ewart Gladstone.

Fetherston was arrested.

He confessed and was amazed at his newfound capacity for remorse.

When he stood on the scaffold he said a silent prayer. At the moment the floor dropped from beneath him and the rope cinched his neck, he experienced a surge of hope—the desperate hope that the redemption of sin was possible, and that the reward was life-everlasting in the hereafter. Preferably, a hereafter that included Emma.

CECIL FETHERSTON'S widow, and their son after her, lived on at the manor house in the Cotswolds.

Succeeding generations of Fetherstons continued to own Rushwood House and The London gallery. The property was always bequeathed to the eldest son. That was the line of succession expected and accepted until Bradford Fetherston.

Shortly before his death, Bradford chose to break tradition for reasons that were made clear to all concerned. Instead of granting title to his only son, Arthur, he named as his heir his daughter, Deborah Foley, née Fetherston.

EIGHT

HENRY MARCH slowed the van as they approached a wrought iron gate that bore an ornate *R* intertwined with an equally decorative *H* for Rushwood House.

Ahead, the taillights of the Volvo disappeared as the driver made a quick left turn, deserting the main gravel road.

"The bloody woman could have left the gate open for us," Henry said.

"I'll get it." Andrea opened her side door as the van came to a stop.

"If you want." Henry shifted to neutral. "But I should protest, shouldn't I?"

"Why?"

"Out of respect for my betters and all that."

"You can practice being civilized once we get there." Andrea jumped down, swung the gate open then closed it behind the van when Henry had driven through.

Around the bend of the narrow road they entered a clearing and saw a bronze fountain in the center of an uneven lawn. The lawn extended to the edges of the encroaching forest and ended on the bank of a small lake that lay in the direction the Volvo had taken.

As Andrea and Henry neared the front of Rushwood House, Arthur Fetherston appeared in a doorway that had been cut through one side of immense double doors. He waved from behind the balustrade of the terrace, then loped down the nearest of the twin stairways that led to the curving drive where a polished black Jaguar and a dusty red Ford Fiesta were parked.

"Hello!" Arthur crossed in front of Henry's van before it had fully stopped. He rested a suede-patched elbow on the ledge of the window as Andrea lowered it. "Miss Perkins, hello." Leaning closer, so that his face was inches from hers, he said, "You're quite as attractive as I remembered. Shall I call you Andrea?"

"Of course." She pulled back slightly and turned to introduce Henry. "Arthur Fetherston, this is my assistant—on loan from the V & A—Henry March."

The two men did not speak but eyed each other briefly—Henry with a smirk, Arthur with a total lack of interest.

"You'd probably like to unload your gear straightaway," Arthur said to Andrea. "Drive through the porte-cochere"—he pointed the way to Henry as though directing a delivery man—"around to the back entrance. I'll go through the house and meet you there."

As the van lurched forward, gravel sprayed Arthur's worsted-woolen trouser legs. With grim satisfaction, Henry said, "A real country gentleman, ain't he?"

"I take it he's not what you consider one of your betters, then?" Andrea got neither word nor smile in response. She hoped she was not going to have to spend the time at Rushwood placating Henry and dodging Arthur.

The room designated as a temporary laboratory was quite large and on the ground floor. There were innumerable shelves and cabinets, a double sink, and a large rectangular table in the center. A huge cast-iron cooking stove stood next to an open-hearth fireplace.

"This was the original kitchen," Arthur explained, "but when my sister became lady of the manor, she converted the pantry into an efficiency-kitchenette sort of thing. The quality of living at Rushwood has shrunk in about the same proportion in every way you can imagine."

He paused to smooth his hair in the small mirror that hung above a metal inset in the wall. A reminder of better days, the panel contained a number of bells and buzzers for summoning servants to various rooms in the house. Tacked beneath it was a diagram of the system on yellowed paper with curling corners. The illegibility of the faded handwritten names and numbers were testimony to the system's long disuse.

"But then, what happens at Rushwood is no concern of mine," Arthur said. "I'm merely a guest here and thank God, I don't have to watch the day-to-day deterioration."

Arthur struck a pose at the side of the fireplace, casually learning against the mantel. "However, I do still take a personal interest in the running of the gallery, though I must say I'm not encouraged to do so."

At the mention of the gallery, Andrea could not help asking, "Do the police have any idea yet who broke into the gallery? It must have been the same person who took the drawing from my desk."

"No. I don't think the police have put either incident very high on their list of crimes to solve."

At that moment, Henry appeared in the doorway carrying two large bottles of distilled water. He asked Andrea where he should put them.

"By the sink." She began to arrange the equipment as Henry brought it in from the van.

Arthur watched the process with interest, but with no offer of assistance. When they had finished, he gave Andrea a hearty "Well done!" as though he had just witnessed a theatrical performance. "I'll show you to your rooms now, and then—one would hope—Deborah can take it from there."

"Arthur!" As if on cue, Deborah swung open the door of the converted pantry. "You should have told me they were here." She managed a gracious smile, but it was obvious that she was annoyed with her brother. "I'm sorry you were brought in through the back, Andrea. Are you finding everything you need?"

"Yes, thank you. We decided to unload first."

Deborah's country-casual skirt and blouse in variegated shades of mauve made Andrea acutely aware of her own jeans and Harvard University sweatshirt. But the lady of the manor—as Arthur called her—was not only dressed for the part of the perfect hostess; she knew how to play the role extremely well.

"We're so grateful that you agreed to come," she said with such warmth and sincerity that the obvious response seemed to be that there was nowhere else in the world that Andrea would rather spend the weekend. Fortunately, no reply was necessary, as Deborah had already turned her attention to Henry. "And this must be the young man you brought along from the V & A." Deborah extended her hand to him. "It's nice to know that the dear old place has the good sense to hire talented young people with enthusiasm and new ideas. New ideas are what's needed to ward off mustiness. And if Andrea has selected you to assist her, you must be just the one we'll be looking to for leadership in the future. Your name is Henry, isn't it?"

"Yes, right. Henry March."

Andrea turned away to hide a grin. Henry had been elevated from pushing a broom to creating policy and was actually blushing at his sudden promotion. He was much better equipped to handle Arthur's rudeness than Deborah's charm.

"I'll be on my way, then," Arthur said. "You can manage, can't you, Debo?"

"I thought you were staying over."

"I'll be back tomorrow, but tonight I'm penciled-in on a dance card at the Savoy." He gave Deborah a quick kiss on the cheek. "And as I'll be driving into London, it seems a good opportunity to give your Jag an airing."

"I don't think so."

Arthur reached toward a metal hook on the wall next to the fireplace. His fingers found nothing there, and a glance confirmed it. "Where's the key?"

"No, Arthur, use your own car."

"It's hardly suitable for the occasion."

"Sorry, but we made an agreement when I bought you the car."

"The real point is, the attendants at the Savoy refuse to park Fords. They're instructed to tell people who have the poor taste to show up in rat-trap economy cars to park them on the street and come back in a cab."

"Don't be absurd." Deborah tried gamely to smile. "Your car is still new."

"New? My God, Deborah. Are you still equating *new* with *desirable*?" Arthur continued to stand where he was near the fireplace, but he turned his back to his sister and spoke directly to Andrea. "You'd think she was born in that horrid place in Florida—Epcot Center. If something is new, Debo thinks it must be just the thing. An example. Here. Right here." He began to walk around the room, flinging his arms about in exaggerated gestures like a petulant child. "Since Rushwood was first built, this room was the kitchen. The only cheerful place in the house, really. With a fire in the fireplace and the smell of bread baking or a joint roasting in the oven, it was a refuge. But once my sister's name was on the property deed, she rang up Harrods and had them ship out a lorry-full of shiny appliances with knobs and buttons and clocks and dials and lined them up in what used to be the pantry and called it a kitchenette.''

Deborah obviously was flustered. ''I don't know how to bake bread, and with no servants about...''

''Is the key in here?'' Arthur stopped his pacing and opened a carved wooden box on the mantel, then began searching through a clutter of tagged keys.

''No.'' Deborah flashed an apologetic smile at Andrea. ''Arthur. I do not want you to take my car.''

He slammed the lid of the box closed. ''Actually, Andrea, my sister has no real appreciation for those drawings of ours that you're here to restore.'' Once again, he deliberately turned his back to his sister. ''They're *old*, you see, and they have dirty, moldy spots on them. Now if you can make them look like illustrations from *Vogue*, she might be interested in keeping them.''

''It's just that I might need the Jaguar before tomorrow,'' Deborah said. ''We're so far from everything out here, and I don't know how to drive a car like yours where you have to shift the gears.''

Deborah had taken a step toward Arthur as she spoke and was looking up at him almost pleadingly, it seemed. Her brother continued to ignore her.

''She—or her husband—may have given you the impression that the Fetherston drawings are solely her property. That is not necessarily the case. Not a proven fact. It is still open to question. There's an interesting legal technicality involved. True, she did inherit the Fetherston Gallery—the windows, the doors, the floors, the ceiling, the plumbing fixtures, the counters, everything attached to the structure—but the *contents*? Ah, yes, what *about* the contents—the things that are not nailed down or screwed in? I'll give her the rats and the spiders—she can keep them, thank you very much—but I've spoken with a solicitor who says that everything else may be open to debate.''

"Arthur..." Deborah reached out and touched his arm.

He shrugged off her hand. "But you're not really interested in that, are you, Andrea, dear? You're just here to ply your trade and, I hope, find some pleasure in the countryside. If I were among the invited guests, I'd see to that aspect of your visit myself."

"You're being tiresome, Arthur." Deborah's voice was low and controlled, but Andrea noticed the slight trembling of her lower lip. "You know you don't need an invitation."

"I really must be getting along." He glanced at his watch and started toward the door to the main part of the house. "Just need to collect a few things from upstairs and be on my way. I will be back tomorrow in my role as part owner of the *contents* of the gallery—at which time I will be pleased to see you again, Andrea." He blew a kiss in her direction. Then, with no acknowledgment of Deborah or Henry, he was out the door, closing it behind him.

After a moment, Deborah made an effort to regain her earlier cheerfulness. "Well, one less place to set for dinner."

"Two, if you were counting me," Henry said.

"Of course I was counting you."

"I thought I'd take a run up to Oxford and visit a school chum. You weren't thinking of starting work on the drawings tonight, were you, Andrea?"

"I suppose not." Actually, she was a bit annoyed. They could have tested the paper to see how stable it was and determined which method of restoration to use. It would have saved some time tomorrow. But Henry was already heading for the door, and Deborah was saying how sorry she was he was leaving.

When he had gone, she said, "Well, Andrea, that leaves just you and me. The others won't be arriving until tomorrow."

"Won't Clayton be here?"

"Not in the flesh. But in about an hour's time we'll see him on television. Some interview program or other. Right now, let's get you settled in your room."

Andrea picked up her suitcase, which Henry had dropped just inside the door, and followed Deborah through a labyrinth of rooms and corridors. The light was too dim to distinguish little more than shapes of chairs and tables and sofas. The odor of furniture polish and dusty draperies hung heavily in the still air. At the top of a carved stairway stretched a long, wide hallway. A light shone from beneath a closed door on the left, and there was the sound of footsteps on a carpeted floor inside. Andrea assumed it must be Arthur collecting his gear. Farther down, on the right, Deborah opened a door and flipped on a wall switch. The bedroom overlooked the lighted fountain.

"This," Deborah said, "is the choice guest room in the house because it has an electric heater that actually works and a large private bath with a tub instead of a stall shower. But there's nothing much else to recommend it, I'm afraid."

"It's lovely." Andrea's sincerity seemed to catch Deborah by surprise.

"Is it? Well, you have an artistic eye and would know better than I, but it has always seemed depressingly barren to me."

The room was quite large with white wainscoting and dark wood paneling. Bare wooden floors were warmed only by a hearth rug and a woven mat at the side of the bed. French doors, a small dressing table between them, opened onto a balcony. There were two chairs in the sparsely furnished room—both confiscated by some previous owner from a queen Anne dining room suite— and a twentieth-century veneer armoire. But the tent bed, Andrea felt, was the real treasure.

The four posts reached halfway up to the high ceiling and supported a curved frame like joists for a roof. The top of the frame was covered, and the sides were hung with a bright green tartan that reached to the floor and enclosed the bed on all four sides. The flaps were tied back on the side facing the fireplace to reveal a bedspread and bolstered pillows in the same cheerful Scots plaid that hung from the frame.

"The bed is rather nice, I suppose." Deborah picked up one of the pillows and fluffed it. "Our infamous forebear, Cecil Fetherston, brought the tartan back from one of his visits with Queen Victoria at Balmoral."

She hugged the pillow to her as she crossed to the obviously new and definitely unsightly electric heater that sat on the hearth and completely blocked a beautiful Georgian fireplace. "The heater has a thermostat, if you'd like to turn it up," Deborah said proudly. "I know you Americans are used to warm rooms."

"It seems fine to me."

"When Arthur and I were growing up, we counted ourselves lucky if we got through the winter without red, spotty legs from chilblains." A little wistfully she said, "We were like twins. Everyone said so, though I'm really a year older. He was such a pretty child... Poor Arthur... It's been hard for him to accept that I inherited Rushwood." She tossed the pillow back on the bed. "Well, there are towels in the bathroom cupboard and an extra blanket on the shelf in the armoire." Smiling from the doorway, she said, "As there will be only the two of us, there's certainly no need to change for dinner."

Andrea laughed. "Your dining room deserves better than these blue jeans."

"No, please don't change. I thought I'd wear jeans, too."

That was hard for Andrea to picture.

"I'm afraid I'm the cook, and if you don't mind, we'll be just 'girls together' in the kitchen."

"Sounds great."

"Our only television set is there, at any rate."

"What is this program you mentioned?"

"It's an interview sort of thing." Deborah glanced at the mantel clock. "If we're to see it from the beginning, we'll have to be downstairs in twenty minutes. Will that be all right with you?"

"I just hope I can find my way," Andrea said, only half joking.

"I'll come back for you in fifteen minutes."

From across the hall there was the sound of a door opening and closing. With a quick wave, Deborah disappeared into the hallway.

"Arthur!"

There was no answer; no sound except for Arthur's footsteps and Deborah's hurrying after him.

"They're in the ignition," Andrea heard Deborah say softly from the top of the stairs. There was silence, then softer still she said, "The keys to the Jaguar are in the ignition."

"Good girl. I thought you'd come around," Arthur said.

Soon after, the front door banged and in less than a minute, Andrea saw the Jaguar round the bend of the curved driveway and disappear among the dark beechwoods.

ARTHUR FETHERSTON could not remember when he first discovered that his sister Deborah feared silence more than anything else. It seemed he had always known. He probably made the discovery as a baby, shortly after he learned that vocal sounds had meaning and produced both positive and negative results.

Like most children, his first and favorite word was *mine*. What joy to say *mine* and point a finger demanding ownership! But to his disappointment, this tactic did not always work. His sister would not always give him her favorite toy, her slice of cake, her turn on the rocking horse. Screams and tears were of no use. They made her more defiant. But silence was magic.

As a toddler, it took no more than pouting lips and pleading eyes. Within a year or two, he learned it was most effective to avert his eyes, to turn his back, to clamp his lips shut and ignore her, sometimes for as long as half an hour. As they grew older, he refined his technique.

If the circumstances of their childhood had been different, Arthur might never have learned to wield this simple weapon with such skill. But while they were still quite young, the special voice—their mother's—that praised and scolded and moderated was lost forever.

Perhaps it was when Arthur saw their father hold Deborah up so that she could see into the casket that he realized the power of silence. Arthur, it was thought, was too young to see his mother in death. But Deborah, though only a year older, was considered more sensitive—she was, after all, a girl—and mature enough to have one last glimpse.

"Mommy, wake up. I'm sorry," the little girl whispered as she looked down at the strange apparition sleeping on the satin pillow.

As with most children, Deborah believed that she was the cause of any effect. Rain or sunshine, sickness or health were the result of her virtue or misdoings. If her mother would not speak to her, it followed that she, Deborah, had done something to deserve this treatment. What? What had she done? What was the unknown transgression that brought on this unbearable punishment of silence?

"Remember how pretty she was, Deborah." Their father's voice was tired—relieved—after months of sleepless nights waiting for the cancer to finally stop the faltering pulse and still the rasp of his wife's breathing.

"I didn't mean to be bad," Deborah mouthed the words.

"The hair's too dark." He reached down and touched the wig that curled—as his wife's never had—across the forehead. "Remember her own hair, sweetheart." He kissed his daughter on the cheek. "Remember how her hair used to shine, how it would crackle with electricity and fly out when she brushed it." Then, for a final symbolic kiss, he placed his daughter's fingers on the lips that were sewn together.

"What did I do, Mommy? Tell me. I won't do it again."

The church was beginning to fill. Their father was too absorbed in his own grief to listen to what his daughter said. He placed little value on the ramblings of children, at any rate. Still holding his daughter and taking the hand of his son, he settled his small family beside him in the pew.

Arthur watched his sister. Deborah was pale and trembling. Her wet eyelashes fluttered and her flickering glance was that of a trapped bird, flying to the stained-glass window, to the stone archway through which the rector entered, to the closed door that led to the churchyard. With the ephemeral understanding of one child for another, Arthur knew that it was not a kiss the little girl wanted from their mother's cold and waxy lips but the sound of her voice. She wanted words of forgiveness for an uncommitted sin.

After the death of their mother, the children had a governess at Rushwood until they were old enough to go to day school. Their father had always spent most of his time in The City and continued to do so. The village of Chipping Codsbury was too far to commute to his office and London was no place for children.

Though both brother and sister had a few school chums, they were not encouraged to invite them home. So Deborah and Arthur spent the long afternoons and evenings and the endless summer vacations with a series of servants. None of the young women of the village who were hired to cook and clean and supervise the children ever stayed long enough to be considered a part of the household. All of them looked on their employment at Rushwood as temporary, a stopgap until they could find permanent jobs in the shops in Chipping Codsbury or office work in Oxford or London.

Boredom was a staple for the two young Fetherstons. Arthur found some amusement in inventing ghosts to inhabit the dark and dusty unused wing of Rushwood. Though Deborah tried to pretend she was frightened by his stories of mysterious, vaporous beings, she was not. She lacked the imagination to believe in anything she could not see. Nor did she have the guile to convince her brother that his elaborate tales were as terrifying as he intended them to be.

Arthur had decided to abandon the ghosts when he hit upon a variation that was more effective than he had ever imagined.

One particularly boring winter day when his sister refused to climb through the skylight in the nursery with him to build a snowman on the roof, he said, "All right, then. You'll be sorry when I'm not here anymore."

"No, I won't."

"Yes, you will. There'll be no one to talk to you."

"You don't say anything worth hearing, anyway."

"I'm warning you, Deborah. I'm going to disappear."

"Are you? Let me see you do it." At last, she seemed interested in what he was saying.

"You can't *see* someone who's disappeared."

"Oh." Deborah turned back to dressing the doll she preferred to Arthur's make-believe adventures.

The truth of his own words confronted Arthur and so he amended his threat. "Actually, you *will* be able to see me. My body will still be here, but I'll be gone."

"Oh." She smiled encouragingly at her brother. Then, deciding that white knee-socks were a better choice to go with the doll's eyelet dress than the brown ones she had put on originally, she set about making the change.

"Everyone else will be able to see me, too. They'll all think I'm still here. You're the only one who will know I'm really gone."

"If that's what you want, Arthur."

"Deborah!"

"What?"

"This is the last time I'm going to tell you."

"What?"

"I'm leaving."

"All right! Leave."

Arthur stood in the middle of the room with his arms stretched out in front of him and rolled his eyes as far back in their sockets as he could manage. First his fingers started to twitch, then his arms, his shoulders, his hips and his legs until his whole body seemed to be vibrating. Finally he collapsed in a chair and his head fell forward on his chest.

Deborah was somewhat impressed by the performance until it stopped. Then, giggling, she grabbed her doll and started for the doorway. "You're still here," she said, and ran out to the sun-room where her doll-house was.

The fact that Arthur did not speak to her at all the rest of the day was rather fun. During dinner, she tried to think of ways to make him talk.

"If you want your pudding, you have to ask for it." She quickly reached for the crystal compote in front of him and held it aloft, waiting for him to yell at her and grab it away. Instead, he went through the baize door into the kitchen and returned with an earthenware cup filled with dessert and took it with him to his room.

By noon the next day, Deborah was weary of the game. It not only made her angry to be in the same room with her brother and to have him ignore her, but it gave her an eerie feeling that she was the one who was invisible.

He was there, she could see him. She would feel the muscle in his arm tighten when she pinched him trying to make him at least cry out in pain. But he had simply shrugged and moved out of her reach without looking at her. He had not allowed their eyes to meet since he announced his disappearance.

As the day wore on, the snow that had stopped after blanketing the house and grounds for two days abruptly began again. The wind was stronger than it had been before. The icy uppermost branches of an oak tree clanked against the dormer windows of the nursery and sudden gusts of chilly air whistled through the space where the skylight did not quite fit the frame.

Finally, Deborah's cold little fingers grasped Arthur's hand and would not let go. "Come back, Arthur," she said. Her eyelashes were wet and fluttering. Though never known for her courage, she looked up at the swirling patterns of snow on the skylight and after a faltering intake of breath, said, "We could go up on the roof and make a snowman—"

Arthur began to laugh.

Deborah was grateful for even that. At least there was some response, some indication that her brother was still inside the scrawny body. "—like you wanted to yesterday. We could climb up through the skylight. Arthur?"

"I'm here," her brother said. Then, looking her full in the face with an exultant grin, "Don't be silly," he said, "it's too windy on the roof. We'd be blown halfway across the county."

NINE

TRUE TO HER WORD, when Deborah returned fifteen minutes later she was wearing jeans. Unlike Andrea's, which were thin at the knees and wrinkled at the hems, Deborah's were pressed and creased. She wore a pale-peach braided belt and a blouse of the same color. Silvery bangles on her wrists clinked together pleasantly as she led the way back downstairs.

The converted pantry at Rushwood House was filled with shiny kitchen equipment in peach-tinted enamel and dazzling chrome. The walls were painted a subdued orange-pink, the same color as Deborah's blouse. Everything was all peaches and chrome, Andrea thought, enjoying her own pun. A combination she felt described Deborah Foley as aptly as it did her kitchen.

"Arthur hates my little converted pantry," Deborah said. "If he had his way, nothing around here would ever change." She began to search through stacks of commercially packaged containers in the freezer. "The poor darling has never forgiven me for inheriting Rushwood and the Fetherston Art Gallery. But, honestly, I was as surprised as he was. I didn't think our father liked *either* of us. Though that didn't enter in when he made out his will, of course." Deborah placed a red-white-and-green-striped package on the counter. She frowned at the box a moment, then returned it to the bottom shelf. "Lasagna's a little heavy, don't you think?"

"Whatever you like is fine," Andrea said.

"Daddy had to name *someone* heir—someone in the family—and I had the advantage of being married to Clayton. 'At least my son-in-law has the American fondness for ownership,' was the way father put it. And it's not as though Arthur were totally cut off. He got the liquid assets—as Clayton calls the money, all of which is probably gone by now."

Deborah emerged from the freezer with a flat cardboard box that featured a picture of dancing mushrooms. "Ah, here it is," she said. "I've always found this Quiche Champignon to be quite good. Is that all right?"

"Sounds great." Andrea was glad for a change of subject. She did not really want to know the details of the strained relationship between Deborah and her brother. "Can I help?"

"No, thank you. I can manage." Deborah began to peel the plastic wrap from the paper box. "I love to cook."

Andrea wanted to laugh but she could see that her hostess was sincere.

"You could move the telly closer to the table, if you would," Deborah said.

"What time is this program Clayton is appearing on?"

The television set was on a kitchen trolley next to the door. Andrea maneuvered it into position.

"Actually, he's already appeared, or rather, it's already been recorded. He said that he was not at all pleased with the show, and that I wouldn't be, either. But he wouldn't say any more than that. Just that we'd talk about it when he got home. I rather chalk it all up to false modesty."

Modesty—false or true—had never been associated with Clayton Foley in Andrea's mind, though she did not mention this to his wife.

"The program is a weekly feature about art-museums, galleries, artists, that sort of thing. This Mandy Carruthers person, the interviewer, tries to make art interesting. She has the credentials—she's something important at the National Gallery and is always throwing her expertise around. And, if all else fails, she leans forward in her inevitable low-cut dress." Deborah glanced at the digital clock above the settings on the microwave oven. "The program should be coming on right about now."

Andrea turned on the set. "What channel?"

". . . here on the 'Art Beat of London,'" a sonorous male voice announced.

"That's it," Deborah said without looking. She stood studying the instructions on the box of quiche.

Andrea decided that her hostess might need some help whether she admitted it or not. Without asking a second time she began to look around for place mats, napkins, plates, and silver.

The television picture locked in on an attractive woman in her thirties. Mandy Carruthers was wearing an emerald green dress with a V-neckline that drew attention to well-shaped breasts but was not low enough to be considered décolleté. Her ash-blond hair was brushed back away from her face. Expert lighting emphasized her high cheekbones and gave her green eyes a sequin-glitter when she looked into the camera.

"Our first guest is a man you have seen many times before," Mandy Carruthers said, "though you may not recognize his name."

A close-up of Clayton Foley filled the screen.

"Oh!" Deborah's voice was ecstatic. "Doesn't he look marvelous?"

The studio makeup gave his rugged features a bronzed sheen. His half-smile and composure—which always seemed studied to Andrea—came across well on television. She glanced at Clayton's wife to agree that, indeed, he did look handsome. But something in the other woman's expression stopped her. Deborah seemed mesmerized. Her face wore the same embarrassing adoration seen on teenage girls in documentaries about rock stars or movie idols.

"In his native America," Mandy continued the introduction. "Mr. Foley did a stint on television as an authority on sport."

"You're much too generous, Mandy," Clayton corrected good-naturedly. "I wasn't exactly an authority, I was a sportscaster.

"At any rate"—Mandy flashed a quick smile toward the camera—"since becoming a Brit by marriage, Clayton Foley is now a familiar presence to all of us as the representative of a clothing manufacturer. You've seen his picture in magazines, in adverts on the sides of buses, and on posterboards in the tube stations, always looking casually handsome in Harris Tweed. And to round out this recital of Mr. Foley's diverse background, we must add that he first came to England as a Rhodes scholar and that his field of study was art history. He was formerly manager of the Fetherston Art Gallery and currently is its owner."

"Forgive me, Mandy," Clayton said, "but my *wife* is actually the owner. The Fetherston Art Gallery has been in her family for several generations. It was started by Cecil Fetherston, who was a somewhat famous artist in his day."

"And somewhat infamous, if I may add."

"He came to a rather inglorious end," Clayton said. Then, grinning, he added, "But I've always thought of the poor guy as just unlucky in love."

"Indeed he was. He was hanged for murdering his mistress."

Deborah had abandoned her cooking and sat at the kitchen table with her guest.

The leisurely pace of the noncommercial outlets on British television still surprised Andrea. Mandy Carruthers's "Art Beat of London" was the sort of esoteric program that would show up five years hence in the midday schedule on American PBS or be shown very late at night by some struggling cable company devoted to the arts.

The microwave timer dinged, and though Andrea glanced in that direction, Deborah took no notice.

"...we called in at the gallery this morning," Mandy was saying as the television picture shifted to a videotaped exterior view of a block of Victorian shops, "and took a look at some of Cecil Fetherston's drawings."

The shops were identical. They all had brick fronts with plaster pilasters and mullioned bay windows that jutted onto the cobbled sidewalk. Mandy Carruthers, now wearing a mink coat the color of dark mahogany, crossed the street and entered the corner establishment. Above the door, a hanging sign announced in Old English script and gold leaf, *Fetherston Gallery of Fine Art*.

The edited videotape shifted to an interior view of the gallery. The single room was of moderate size. All the available wall space was filled with framed oil paintings, watercolors, pencil or pen-and-ink drawings, and delicate pastels. The technique and subject matter of the pictures suggested that none of them had been completed earlier than a hundred years ago.

In an alcove, a silver tea service sat atop a gate-legged table. At each side were bobbin-turned chairs. Mandy, minus her coat and wearing a yellow plaid dress with a V-neck, was in the chair at the left. On the right was a woman in her mid-thirties who wore a tobacco-colored dress; her brown hair was arranged in a French twist. Her makeup looked pale in comparison with Mandy's, but her large eyes were deep-set and naturally shadowed, their intensity suggesting that she had little need for the magnifying glass and jeweler's loupe that hung from antique gold chains around her neck.

"There's Sybil!" Deborah smiled delightedly at the television screen. "I didn't know Sybil was going to be interviewed."

Andrea asked, "Who's she?"

"Sybil Forbes. She manages the gallery. You'll meet her tomorrow night."

The gallery manager answered Mandy's questions concerning Cecil Fetherston's history discreetly. She did not add any elaborating detail. As she spoke, she took four of the artist's drawings from a portfolio at the side of her chair and placed them carefully—one behind the other—on an easel for the camera.

Andrea stood and moved closer to the television set. This was the first time there had been an opportunity to examine the drawings, except for a brief glance at the one that had been stolen from her desk.

The first portrait to fill the screen was of William Gladstone, looking stern and pious as chancellor of the exchequer. Next was Queen Victoria in her early forties, voluptuous and regal as portrayed by the artist. The third was a sadly wan but handsome Prince Albert, sketched—so Sybil Forbes, the manager of the gallery explained—less than a year before his death. And the fourth drawing was of the dour and rugged highlander, John Brown.

All the drawings seemed to be in fairly good condition. Andrea thought, though they each bore the reddish brown fox marks she had seen on the one that had been stolen.

"Have you had any word from the police," she asked Deborah.

"The police?"

"About the drawing that was stolen. Have they made any headway at all in finding it?"

"Oh. No, I don't think so." Almost as an afterthought she added, "Fortunately, the picture you had was the least valuable of the lot." Deborah had abandoned the television set for the refrigerator. She had little interest in the program unless her husband was onscreen. "I'm afraid tinned pineapple and Stilton are all I can find to go with the quiche."

The camera was still holding on the portrait of John Brown. Mandy Carruthers was giving a brief biography of Queen Victoria's Highland servant, ladling on innuendo about the relationship between the two.

"Thank heaven it wasn't 'The Balmoral Nude' that was stolen," Deborah said over the whirr of the electric can opener. "That's the one that Clayton says is the most valuable."

"Who is the nude?"

"It's not just one, actually, but two."

"Two drawings?"

"No. Two people. Two figures in the same drawing."

Suddenly, a close-up of Clayton appeared on television again, and Deborah sloshed pineapple juice on the counter in her hurry to sit down and watch.

". . . the drawings have suffered from old age and dampness," Clayton was saying, "but we're having them restored."

The camera dollied back to reveal Mandy and Clayton, as before, seated in the studio behind a coffee table.

Mandy leaned forward to pick up a sheaf of notes and gave the camera a shadowed shot of cleavage. Straightening, she said, "Mr. Foley, you are acquainted, I believe, with Lord and Lady Wesley Smith-Hamilton, the owners of a private museum in Phoenix, Arizona."

"Yes, they've made purchases from our gallery on several occasions."

"So they told us. Indeed, they indicated that they were currently in London specifically to close an interesting transaction with the Fetherston Gallery."

The camera registered a slight chink in Clayton Foley's composure in the form of a perplexed frown before cutting away to a videotape of an expensively decorated living room in the Knightsbridge Club.

Lord and Lady Smith-Hamilton were seated on a curved sofa in front of a marble fireplace where a fire blazed cheerfully around gas logs.

The Smith-Hamiltons were a strikingly handsome middle-aged couple. They both had well-coiffed gray hair, set off to good advantage by Arizona suntans. Diamonds of inordinate size sparkled on the fingers of Lady Smith-Hamilton.

Mandy Carruthers was seated in an armchair to one side of the couple. For this segment of the program the interviewer wore a blue wraparound dress, and when she leaned forward to question Lord Smith-Hamilton, one partially exposed breast gleamed whitely in the firelight. "You maintain your suite here at the Knightsbridge Club year-round, isn't that so, Lord Smith-Hamilton?"

"Yes, but I'm afraid we don't see much of it."

"How often do you get to London from Phoenix?"

"Not damned often enough to pay for this place. For the same price we could rent the whole Ritz Hotel for the time we're here."

Lady Smith-Hamilton laughed pleasantly, then added, "Don't listen to him. We're here fairly often. At least twice a year. We come over to go to the auction houses and galleries and to be with our daughter, who is at a design school near Oxford." Lady Smith-Hamilton indicated an oil painting above the fireplace. "That's our daughter, India."

The portrait was painted in shades of beige and brown with swirling brushstrokes of raw umber for the lustrous hair which framed an oval face. The girl appeared to be in her late teens. Her pouting mouth was brick red and her chestnut-umber eyes looked back insolently from the canvas.

"The Smith-Hamiltons are rather nice," Deborah said. She removed the quiche from the microwave oven and placed it on a chrome platter. "But that daughter of theirs is a real trial. They bought their title just for her."

"Oh, yes. You mentioned that they *bought* their title." Andrea crossed to the counter to pick up the two salad plates with their soupy pineapple slices and crumbling chunks of Stilton. "How?"

"At an auction on Painter's Street in the financial district, just as if it were a china cat or a pewter mug."

"I didn't know that was possible."

"These days, most of the British aristocracy is willing to sell anything if the price is right. Most of the land has already been sold. So have the grand houses. And, of course, the servants are gone. All that's left are the titles—which were bequeathed, thus transferable..."

"...and thus, salable," Andrea added.

"That's the way it is, I'm afraid."

Andrea watched Lord Smith-Hamilton chatting with Mandy Carruthers about his interest in Victorian art. He seemed such an obvious product of the American West, with his silver collar-points and his turquoise bolo tie. What would he want with an English title, Andrea wondered. But of course, Deborah was right. It was probably his wife and daughter who wanted it. "What goes *with* the title, what can they do with it?"

"Usually nothing goes with it," Deborah said as she sliced the pallid-looking quiche into wedges. "No land or anything. They might have the right to graze sheep on the village common or something like that. But all they can do with it, actually, is have business cards engraved or have 'Lord or Lady Smith-Hamilton' printed on their passports or American Express cards. Their names will be listed in Debrett's *Peerage*, but not among the true blue bloods." Deborah suddenly turned to Andrea with a rare look of determination. "I'm not going to sell Rushwood," she said.

"I didn't know you were considering it," Andrea said, surprised.

"I know about the taxes and upkeep and all that." Deborah seemed to be debating with someone other than Andrea. "But a hundred thousand tourists pay to go through some of the stately homes each year. It's true that the architecture of Rushwood isn't outstanding enough to attract much interest, and the gardens have all gone to seed, but with the Fetherston drawings..."

"...with the Fetherston drawings," Lady Smith-Hamilton spoke the same words at almost the same time as Deborah, shocking Andrea and her hostess into giving their full attention to the television program again.

"You think, then," Mandy Carruthers was saying, "that the drawings would round out your collection?"

"They tie in very well with what we have already," Lady Smith-Hamilton said. "As my husband said, we first became interested in Victorian art because of Landseer's famous painting. You know the one where Queen Victoria is pictured seated on a horse while the reins were being held by her Scottish man-Friday—or whatever he was to her."

"John Brown, again," Mandy offered.

"It seemed to me," Lady Smith-Hamilton said, "that there must have been something going on if she had a portrait painted of the two of them together."

"Bessie liked the idea of scandal in the Landseer picture," Wesley Smith-Hamilton said, "and I liked the way he painted the horse."

"I swear, Wesley, you and your damned horses." Bessie Smith-Hamilton was smiling, but obviously only because she was aware of the red light on the camera. "Mandy, you can't believe how many Victorian paintings of horses we have."

"But you were saying about the Fetherston drawings..." Mandy Carruthers made an attempt to draw the Smith-Hamiltons back to the original subject.

"Yes." Bessie Smith-Hamilton's smile was genuine now. "At last we have been able to buy something I really want."

Her husband said cautiously, "Bessie, I'm not sure you should mention that yet."

"We've got it in writing." Lady Smith-Hamilton picked up a square envelope from the end table next to the couch. Her diamonds flashed as she tapped the envelope on the back of her hand. "Mandy," she said, "we've made offers before, but the Fetherston Gallery has finally agreed to sell us their entire collection of Cecil Fetherston drawings."

"They're not actually in our possession yet, Bessie."

"No, but we have an agreement to sell that is signed by Deborah Fetherston Foley."

Andrea was aware of everything that happened. It just took some sorting out. She was so intrigued by Lady Smith-Hamilton's statement that they had purchased the Fetherston drawings, that she barely noticed Deborah Foley's sharp intake of breath. Somewhere, far beyond that, she heard a shuffling sound—footsteps?—from behind the door that led into the original Rushwood kitchen where Andrea had set up her workroom.

But for the moment, everything else was lost in the sound of a loud metallic crash behind her.

Andrea turned in time to see Deborah drop the chrome platter on the counter. The platter pivoted at an angle that sent the quiche skidding off the edge and splattering on the floor like globs of wet plaster.

TEN

DEBORAH DID NOT SEEM to notice that the platter had slipped from her hands. Her face had turned white. "It's not true," she said. "I never agreed to sell!"

Part of the ill-fated quiche had splattered on the breakfast bar next to Andrea. Little grease spots dotted both her Harvard sweatshirt and the peach-colored blouse of her hostess.

"So you will be taking the Fetherston drawings back to your gallery in Phoenix," Mandy Carruthers was saying.

"And the sooner the better," Lord Smith-Hamilton replied. "I'm ready for some damned Arizona sunshine again."

"That is not a bill of sale!" Deborah pointed a finger at the television screen where an envelope appeared in Lady Smith-Hamilton's hand. "There's nothing binding about that. It's only a courtesy letter. I don't even know where she got it. *I* didn't send it."

Clayton Foley's face again filled the television screen. His expression was one of baffled amusement.

When Mandy Carruthers began to speak, the camera angle changed to include her and reveal the studio set once again.

"Have we happened upon an exclusive bit of news here, Mr. Foley? Will the Fetherston drawings be leaving with Lord and Lady Smith-Hamilton?"

Clayton cleared his throat before answering and managed a smile when he said, "Of course my wife—

just like everyone else's—doesn't always tell me everything. But this is the first I've heard of any agreement to sell."

"Clearly, there is some misunderstanding, as we have *another* view of the ultimate destination of Cecil Fetherston's work." Mandy shifted slightly in her chair and spoke directly to the camera in the crisp manner of a newscaster. "The following interview is with writer Malcolm Putney concerning his soon-to-be-published biography of William Gladstone."

The establishing shot of the videotape that followed was of the interior of a small, cluttered office. Malcolm Putney was seated at a desk in front of an untidy bookcase.

Putney was a tall, slim man in his early forties. His sandy hair was trimmed close around the neck and ears but left long on top, and kept falling across his forehead. Because of this, he had a habit of tilting his chin back as he spoke and combing through his hair with long, slender fingers. His mustache was several shades darker than his hair, which led one to wonder if he tinted either or both. He was wearing a pastel blue sweater that accentuated the knobbiness of his shoulders and the sharpness of his elbows, which were propped on the desktop.

The room was too small to include Mandy in the picture. Presumably, she was seated across the desk. The interview began with the usual inane greetings and a list of the writer's previous credits which led to Mandy's saying, "Mr. Putney, your publisher promises that not only the text but the illustrations of your novel will shed new light on the life and times of Mr. Gladstone."

"As you've been kind enough to inquire about my book," Putney said, "it seems niggling of me to start off correcting you."

"Oh? Where was my mistake?"

"This is *not* a novel but an autobiography."

"Your publisher calls it a novel."

Putney answered with a superior smile. "That's a little disclaimer the publishing house insisted on. The book, however, is written in the first person as Gladstone would have told his own story had he not been so repressed."

"How did you come to that conclusion?"

"It's perfectly obvious," Putney answered. "The poor man was so fraught with feelings of guilt brought on by his sexual obsession that he was left all but speechless."

"I thought he was one of the more eloquent speakers of the day."

"Oh, yes. He had no problem stating his views on public matters. It's all documented—his lowering of taxes, his plumping for Irish home rule to no avail. All his good works are in the written record. It's the unwritten that I find so fascinating."

"For example?"

Putney jerked his head back and combed his hair with a flurry of fingers. "His penchant for consorting with prostitutes, of course..."

"That's fairly well known, too. Gladstone acknowledged it himself and said he was merely interested in saving their souls."

"So he said," Putney commented with what could only be described as a smirk. "But the real revelation of my book is deep antipathy between Gladstone and our sainted Victoria."

"There again," Mandy said unkindly, "that's well-covered ground. Their dislike for each other was hardly a secret."

Putney looked flustered. "Perhaps, but I dare say you'll find my account of their feud more lively than others. And there's one section of my book that will surprise even you, Ms. Carruthers."

"Oh? What's that?"

"The illustrations. Some drawings by an artist named Cecil Fetherston have recently surfaced. His talent was not wholly remarkable, but he did, nevertheless, have the admiration of the queen." Putney hurried on, talking too fast. "She, of course, was not known for her artistic taste—evidenced by the fact that she was also a great admirer of P. T. Barnum and his "General" Tom Thumb. Not to mention her fondness for Charles Dickens's novels. But no matter. Fetherston was her tutor as well as her confidant."

The camera took notice of Putney's nervousness as he spoke by briefly focusing on his hands. He moved an onyx pen stand on his desk an inch to the left, he righted a bottle of Liquid Paper that had fallen on its side, he picked up a pencil and tapped the eraser end on his palm.

"Oh, my God." Deborah Foley moved closer to the television screen.

Andrea was puzzled. "What is it?"

"Look. Tucked in the edge of the blotter on his desk."

A cream-colored envelope with a distinctive blue seal embossed on the flap—twin to the one Lady Smith-Hamilton had held—was clearly visible.

The camera pulled back to a medium shot to include Putney's face. "...I have been given exclusive permission to include the drawings from the Fetherston collection in my book. One, in particular, will astound my readers.''

Mandy asked, ''What is so astounding about it?''

''My dear, at the price my publisher plans to ask for this tome, I can hardly reveal that. You, like everyone else, must buy a copy to find out. However, I will tell you that I have entitled the illustration 'The Balmoral Nude.' ''

''He *did* ask for the drawings,'' Deborah said. ''I thought it might be a good idea to let him use them in his book, but we've never actually given him permission.''

Andrea asked, ''What's in those envelopes he and the lady from Arizona have?''

''Nothing important. They're courtesy letters we send from the gallery once a transaction has been completed. There are a stack of them that are already signed that stay in the desk. But I didn't send either one of those...'' Deborah's explanation trailed off.

Both women sat silently watching Malcolm Putney as he described the years of research that had gone into the writing of his book.

Then Mandy Carruthers returned to the screen to sum up the evening's program and preview the feature for the following week.

When it was clear that Clayton's appearance was concluded, Deborah switched off the television set. ''Forgive me, Andrea,'' she said. ''I'm going upstairs and see if I can track down my brother on the telephone. I think I know how this all came about.''

Andrea was left staring after her hostess, then at the quiche on the floor.

ELEVEN

HE WAS FIRST to step out of the shower. "Hurry, darling," he said. "There's something we need to talk about."

To hurry was the last thing she wanted. Languorously, she rubbed shampoo into her hair a second time, then stood under the full force of the steaming water, feeling the soapy foam slither down her body.

"Come on! It's important!"

Reluctantly, she turned off the faucet but still made no move to leave. Standing with her eyes closed, she enjoyed a feeling of lassitude as the sweet-scented steam still swirled around her. But the shower's warmth was gone almost instantly. The water that dripped from her wet hair collected in a stream down the indentation of her spine and was icy by the time it reached her buttocks. Shivering, she opened the glass door of the shower stall, releasing ghostly forms of vapor that rose and disappeared as she stepped onto the bath mat.

With her eyes still closed, she waited for him to wrap her in a towel—to kiss her neck—to touch her body in unexpected places.

"I'm cold," she said. "It's cold in here."

She heard his breathing but was not sure where he was in the small room until his hands lightly clasped the tops of her shoulders from behind. Tilting her head down, she kissed the fingers of his right hand, then closed her lips around a second knuckle and gently bit the skin.

"No," he said, almost sharply.

He lifted her chin with the backs of both hands, holding her head as straight and high as though she wore a brace. With his thumbs, he massaged the tendons behind her ears. She murmured her pleasure and leaned back toward him. Slowly, his grasp widened. His thumbs were at the base of her skull and fingers curved around her throat, pressing—gently, but with sufficient strength that she could not turn her head.

"Don't." Her eyes flew open and she tried to see his reflection in the mirror on the bathroom door, but it was fogged over.

"Could you do this?" His chin rested on the top of her head and his voice was little more than a whisper. "If there was no danger of being caught, could you put all your strength in your hands and do this?" His hold on her throat tightened briefly, uncomfortably, then loosened. But he did not let go.

"Don't."

"Could you?"

"Let me go."

"No one would suspect you."

"Stop!"

"Could you?"

"No!"

"You *could*, you know. You're strong. All that running and jogging has given you wonderful muscles."

She had guessed that murder was what he had in mind all along. What she had not known until now was that he intended that *she* should be the murderer.

"It would be fast and easy."

"No."

One person was already dead because of her. She had killed that girl outside Claridge's. No. Not true. The *taxi* killed the girl. That girl *fell* in front of the taxi. But...

"It would be dark. It would be easy—if it were a surprise—if you came from behind like this."

What she had felt about the girl, surprisingly, was not remorse. She had a flashing memory of sitting on the bench in Hyde Park all but paralyzed with fear—fear that someone had seen her. Gradually, she had realized that no one had, and finally, she felt a strange sort of elation—like that of being the only survivor of a plane crash.

"You know you could do it."

"Let go of me." Panic suddenly swept through her. She grabbed at his hands and tried to tear his fingers loose.

"That's right," he said. "That's exactly what will happen. But you can't let go. You'll have to hold even tighter."

His grip was unbreakable. Clumsily, she tried kicking backward at him. He dodged or had moved back beyond her reach. With a final, swift squeeze of his fingers that seemed to blind her and force clicking sounds from her throat, he let go.

Her legs began to crumple. He caught her under the arms and stood her upright.

She made a whimpering sound and steadied herself. Then, clenching her fist—her arm straight—she whirled and struck him with all her strength in the side of the rib cage.

He laughed. "I didn't really hurt you, did I?"

She did not answer. Instead, she pushed her wet hair back from her forehead and glared at him.

Gently, he took her hands in his and kissed the palms. Then, reaching toward a clothes hook on the wall, he took the belt from her robe and tied it loosely around her, pinning her arms to her sides. He lifted her off the floor so that their faces were level and her feet were dangling at the middle of his shins. "Just one more thing, my love," he said. "You know what a garrote is, don't you?"

"Yes."

He kissed the corner of her mouth. "A garrote would be easier to use than bare hands. Something like this belt of yours, or a scarf. It would be neater and faster. And, if you had a handful of cotton with a little ether sprinkled on it—if you used that first, then there'd be no noise and no scuffling." He kissed the other side of the mouth.

No, is what she meant to say, but he covered her mouth with his before she could speak. She tried for a moment to turn her head away. Then her arms worked free, and she draped them across his shoulders.

Lifting her higher, he kissed her neck where his fingers had been. "I didn't hurt you, did I?"

"No. But I didn't like it."

"Well, the lesson's over." He loosened his grip and let her slide slowly down his body until her feet touched the floor. "Now, let's do something you *will* like."

She leaned against him, her face buried in his chest. There was still time to say no. There was still time to think of another way. She would be the one taking all the risk. He could even walk away when it was over and leave her with nothing.

He kissed her lightly on the top of the head.

She did not move.

Holding her by the shoulders, he stepped back and waited until she looked into his eyes. "It's the only way," he said. "They'd suspect me first thing. You know you have to be the one to do it, don't you?"

She was shivering again. Her wet hair was plastered to her head and a cold trickle of water inched down her spine. "Yes, I know." She raised her arms to him.

TWELVE

ANDREA FOUND THAT sleeping in the tent bed at Rushwood House was like sleeping in a plaid-lined cave. She had spent the night curled in a ball like a hibernating animal with only her nose exposed to the elements. And the elements seemed free to come and go as they pleased. The white curtains rippled in front of windows where spaces around the warped frames allowed the cold wind to enter. As Andrea uncovered one eye, she could even see a faint dusting of snow on the inside sill. A respectable icicle had formed on the latch that locked the mullioned windows together. If, as Deborah Foley had told her, this was the warmest of the guest rooms, she could scarcely imagine what the others were like.

The electric heater on the hearth served no purpose at all, as far as she could tell. Its flat, gray planes and curved corners seemed to be merely an art deco intrusion into a lovely Victorian room.

As a delaying tactic for leaving the small circle of warmth that her body generated under the weight of three blankets, she imagined what it must have been like to be a guest in this room when Cecil Fetherston owned Rushwood House.

The window frames probably fit tightly against the cold wind, for one thing, and there would have been a wood fire blazing in the fireplace. Someone from belowstairs would have seen to that.

About now, there should be a discreet knock on the door. A young housemaid with downcast eyes would enter. She would be wearing floor-length black and a starched white apron and cap and would be carrying a footed silver tray.

"Your breakfast, Miss." There would be a steaming pot of tea, a linen napkin in a silver ring, a bone-china cup and saucer so delicate that you could see your fingers through them, and a matching plate kept warm beneath a silver dome.

"Cook wasn't sure you'd care for kippers—you being American, and all," the maid would say, "so the grounds keeper cut a hole in the ice on the lake and caught a fresh trout for you. But if that's not to your taste, there's sausage and bacon, too, and the gardener sent up one of his prize tomatoes from the hothouse to go with the eggs. You do like fried tomatoes, don't you, Miss?" Whereupon, the maid would lift the dome from the plate and release an absolute symphony of aromas.

Warmed by this fantasy, Andrea bravely stretched her cramped legs down through the frigid bedclothes. Suddenly, she made contact with something cold and slick and soft. Repulsed, she jerked her foot back, then realized it was the hot-water bottle—no longer hot—that Deborah had given her to warm the sheets before she got into bed.

Unwelcome reality propelled her to her feet and into her corduroy jeans and bulky knit sweater as quickly as her cold fingers could manage the buttons and zippers and hooks. All the while she mourned the loss of braziers of live coals to warm the bed at night and the open fires to greet the guest in the morning.

No more housemaids, she thought as she struggled into her stiff leather boots. No more parlor maids, cooks, grounds keepers, gardeners, footmen, and Lord knows how many other servants Cecil Fetherston might have employed.

There were neither warming fires not friendly servants at the manor now. All were gone, and for good and just reasons.

To protect the environment, many parts of Great Britain were designated as smokeless zones—one of which included the Fetherston property. As a result, logs no longer crackled and blazed in the fireplaces, and the giant kitchen stove rusted from disuse because smoke from burning wood and coal polluted the air. As to servants, there were none to be had. Being "in service" was now considered demeaning, and, therefore, the salary requirements were prohibitive. So the house remained cold and untended. The British Commonwealth undoubtedly was the better for change. Unfortunately, the same was not true of Rushwood House.

According to Deborah Foley, the pink and white van of the Cotswold Cleaning Service arrived twice a month and "It costs the earth just to have three surly women move the dust around." When the Foleys entertained, the King's Table Catering Company was called upon. Otherwise, they coped in the peaches-and-chrome converted pantry.

Andrea hurried down the musty hallway toward the back stairs. She was hungry. After the disaster of the quiche the night before, dinner—finally—had been canned vegetable soup.

She hoped at least to find bread to make toast and—please, God—some coffee.

What she did find surprised her. Clayton Foley stood at the microwave oven carefully lining up slices of bacon on a paper towel-lined plate. Incongruously, he was wearing plus fours, knee-socks, polished brogues, a wool vest, checked shirt, and knitted tie. A herringbone tweed jacket hung on the back of a kitchen chair, and in the seat lay a cartridge belt and a flat woolen cap. A hunting rifle was propped against the chair.

Andrea laughed. This was not the Clayton Foley she had known. She remembered him in faded jeans and a football jersey. "You're a perfect picture of the country squire at home."

"Good morning." Grinning at her, he hooked a thumb in the watch pocket of the vest. "A bit much, isn't it?"

"What's with the gun?" She perched on the bar stool at the end of the counter. "Do you really go out stylishly tramping through the woods and shooting small creatures?"

"I've been known to. But this getup is for a magazine photo session."

He put the bacon in the microwave and set the timer. "I knew you'd be up early," he said, reaching for the Silex coffee pot. He filled an orange plastic mug and set it in front of her. "I remember that about you," he said. "You always crawled out of bed early, looking a little puffy-eyed and disheveled and panting for coffee."

"None of that, Clayton," she said sternly.

"Sorry." After a moment he added, "At least this morning your hair is combed."

Andrea let the comment pass, though she resented it. He had no right to remember something that personal about her. At least, he had no right to mention it here in his wife's kitchen.

"The photographer wanted to take some shots down by the lake," Clayton said. "The advertising copy reads something like, 'Inside every pin-striped businessman is a sportsman longing for tweeds.' Do you think it will sell?''

"Whatever you put your hand to seems to sell, according to Mandy Carruthers.''

"Oh, yes. You saw the television show last night.''

"Your wife was quite upset.''

"So she told me.''

The bell on the microwave dinged. Clayton removed the bacon and set the plate on the kitchen bar between them. "Do you want an egg? Toast?''

"Toast would be nice.''

He put two thin-cut slices of bread in the chrome toaster, then refilled both their mugs. "No butter, right?''

"Right.''

When the toast popped up, he handed her one piece and took a large bite from the other. With their fingers, they both picked up strips of bacon from the single plate and ate them. Just the way we used to, Andrea thought.

Suddenly self-conscious, she asked, "What was that all about last night? Both the couple from Arizona and that Putney character claiming they had bought the Fetherston drawings?''

"It's all been cleared up now. Fortunately, I was able to get in touch with Putney and the Smith-Hamiltons immediately after that God-awful program and explain to them—with considerable fawning and apologizing—that the drawings have not been sold to anyone, yet.'' A fleeting look of irritation crossed Clayton's face. "And according to what my wife said to me this morning, they never will be.'' The irritation became an exasperated laugh. "But that's merely her decision of the day—who knows what the morrow may bring?''

It was the second time Clayton had implied that his wife was a bit dotty. Andrea had not gotten that impression of Deborah. She might be a bit indecisive—there was that business about Arthur's borrowing her Jaguar. She had said no, then given in, and he had driven away in it. But last night when she'd confided to Andrea that she was going to keep the drawings here on display and open Rushwood to tourists, it sounded like a plan to which she had given a great deal of thought.

"But at least we don't have a lawsuit to worry about," Clayton said. "Neither Putney nor the Smith-Hamiltons had a legal contract."

"Then what was the big to-do about the envelopes?"

Clayton refilled their coffee cups. "The gallery—since Cecil Fetherston's day—has sent a courtesy note to clients, signed by the owner, once a sale has been consummated. It's true that they should not have been sent to Putney *or* the Smith-Hamiltons," he said darkly, "and I'm not sure *who* is responsible for that slip-up, but in any case, it's all merely embarrassing, not legally binding. Here," he said, "I'll show you." He reached beneath the breakfast bar for his briefcase and pulled out a square envelope identical to the ones that had been shown the night before on television. He handed it to Andrea.

Inside was a card on which was written in elegant cursive:

Congratulations on Your Recent Purchase
from the Fetherston Gallery.
"All passes. Art alone
Enduring stays to us;
The Bust outlasts the throne,—

The Coin, Tiberius."
Ars Victrix.

May you and your future generations enjoy——

The next line was left blank to be filled in with the title of the work of art the customer had purchased. Below that, the card read, "Sincerely yours,"—and the signature—"Deborah Fetherston Foley."

Andrea handed the card back to Clayton. She asked, "Was the blank filled in on the cards sent to Putney and Their Lordships?"

"Oh, yes. Both cards read, 'May you and your future generations enjoy the entire collection of original Cecil Fetherston drawings—numbers one through seventeen.'"

Andrea sipped her coffee without comment.

"There's a stack of notes at the gallery," Clayton said, "all pre-signed. Deborah called Sybil early this morning to see if she had sent the ones to Putney and the Smith-Hamiltons by mistake, but apparently she's as mystified as we are."

"Sybil—the manager of the gallery?"

"Yes. Sybil Forbes."

Sybil was not the one Deborah suspected was responsible, Andrea thought. At least, it was not Sybil whom Deborah had spent an hour trying to reach on the phone when the television program was over; it was Deborah's brother, Arthur.

Andrea asked, "Who else works at the gallery?"

"We have a couple of part-timers, a guard, and," Clayton added stoically, "Arthur is on the payroll."

Andrea ate the last crumb of bacon from the plate between them and reached for a paper napkin from a silvery latticework holder. "Thanks for the break-fast," she said.

She was not here to get involved in a family squab-ble, she reminded herself. She was here to restore a set of nineteenth-century drawings that as yet, she had not even seen. She stood to leave. "I'd like to start work now, if you'll get the drawings for me."

"Sure." Clayton reached into his briefcase again and took out a heavy cardboard folder encased in an air-tight plastic bag.

Plastic, for heaven's sake, Andrea thought. The Fetherston drawings should not have been put in plas-tic unless they were totally free of moisture. No won-der there seemed to be so much foxing.

"These are the four that were shown on Mandy Car-ruthers's show last night. Will they be enough to get you started until I finish with the photographer?"

"I suppose the whole set is in pretty much the same condition?"

"I think so."

"Then, yes," Andrea answered. "These should tell me what sort of treatment they'll require so that I can get set up." She took the package from him and turned to go to the old kitchen, which was set up as her labo-ratory.

"Hey, Red!" Clayton took a step toward her. "You still look great first thing in the morning." He put his hands on her shoulders and kissed her lightly on the cheek. "It's good to see you again."

She gave him a half-smile, a nod, and a nervous little wave of the hand as she went through the door.

It was a perfectly proper thing for him to do, she told herself.

Still, there was no excuse for his "first thing in the morning" line. That was taking unfair advantage. It had been a long time since there had been a "first thing in the morning" between them.

She placed the plastic package on the worktable and removed the cardboard envelope.

He still wears the same after-shave lotion, she thought.

THIRTEEN

THOUGH HENRY MARCH had told Andrea he planned
to spend the night in Oxford with friends, he had no
such intention. Instead, he whiled away the greatest part
of the evening at the nearest pub, The Bugle Horn.
There, he drank a couple of pints of Guinness, ate a
passable shepherd's pie, and played darts with the locals. At closing time, he headed back in the direction
from which he had come. He reentered the gates to
Rushwood House and parked out of sight in a thicket
on the opposite side of the lake where he spent the rest
of the frigid night in a sleeping bag inside his van.

The fact that he had said he would do one thing and
had done something quite different was not because he
was devious or secretive by nature. Indeed, most people thought his fault lay in the other direction. He was
much too quick to say exactly what he thought about
everything and his opinions were invariably in opposi-
tion to the status quo. But one topic he had never discussed at any length with anyone—not even with
Andrea in the long, companionable hours they had
spent together in the workroom of the Victoria and Albert Museum—was his passion for bird-watching. He
was, to his great chagrin, an incurable bird-watcher.

A bird-watcher, to Henry and his friends, was the
type of character depicted in a *Punch* cartoon. A bird-
watcher typified the totally—and traditionally—and
eccentrically British middle-class bumbler. And a bird-
watcher was fathoms and leagues from the picture of

the nonconformist radical that Henry liked to present of himself. Still, there it was.

The previous afternoon he had seen a pair of whooper swans and several pintail ducks on the lake, which suggested that there might be even more interesting waterfowl nearby. He could not resist the opportunity to have an early morning look around to see what other winged creatures he might spot.

Henry had grown up in Nottingham in the semidetached house of his parents. His father was a lorry driver whose regular route was from London to Leeds and back on the M1. The senior March's cargo varied but often included kitchen appliances.

When Henry was ten, he confiscated a discarded packing crate from the back of the lorry. The cardboard container had once held a washing machine. It was perfect, he decided, for the walls and ceiling of a tree house. He had already constructed the wooden floor between two sturdy branches of a backyard oak. On one side of the inverted box he cut an arched doorway that he could crawl through. In each of the other three sides he punched out a peephole.

The world was infinitely more interesting to Henry as seen from inside that washing machine carton. He thought of himself as a spy as he crouched undetected in the stuffy box peering through a jagged hole.

He watched the progression of ants as they trailed single-file up the uneven bark. He studied a spider on a leaf. Then he studied the oak leaf itself and wondered why it was shiny on top and dull on the underside and if all the tiny veins were really necessary. Most intriguing of all, however, were the birds.

The secretive hawfinch, for instance, was seldom seen from ground level. Its camouflage colors of beige and black were lost in the brownish shadows of leaves. In his tree house, the young Henry was able to watch at close range while the bird with its outsized bill broke open acorns as easily as Henry unwrapped a candy bar.

But it was the flamboyant green woodpecker that made him catch his breath in wonder. Once, from only inches away, he watched this largest of the native British woodpeckers clamp its claws into a perpendicular limb and brace its tail against the tree for extra support as it foraged beneath the bark. Henry was so close he could distinguish each brilliant green feather and inspect the density of the fine, red fuzz on the crown of the bird's head. He could see the rounded chest flutter with each heartbeat and hear the tiny tapping sounds as the bird dug a beetle from the bark. Once the meal was finished, the woodpeckers's, loud ringing cry, sounding like insane laughter, sent terror coursing through Henry as though he, too, were a member of the insect world and might be the predator's next victim.

The spectacle of what seemed to him a previously undiscovered life-form filled the boy with inexpressible awe. He was unable to describe—even to himself—exactly how he felt, and so he never mentioned it to anyone else.

Long after the rain had turned his cardboard tree house to pulp, he still secretly enjoyed watching the birds from afar. As he grew older, he saved his money and purchased a pair of binoculars. When he went away to school, he occasionally bought books about birds from a second-hand bookseller in Bloomsbury. But now that he had chosen the indoor career of art restoration, he seldom had an opportunity to see anything other than the city pigeons and dusty sparrows that flocked around the square near where he lived.

It was little wonder then, seeing the ducks and swans on the Rushwood lake, and realizing what a great variety of bird life might reside there, that he could not resist the temptation.

During the night, Henry had been awakened several times by the sound of an ice-laden tree branch scraping against the roof of the van and once by a light that flashed somewhere off to the left. At first he thought it must be the headlights of another automobile driving along the same narrow road he had taken, but that seemed unlikely. Why would anyone else be there that late at night? The rutted road led nowhere but to the edge of the lake. He decided that what he had seen was a flash of lightning and went back to sleep with the unhappy thought that probably either heavy rain or snow would be arriving soon.

At the first grayish trace of morning, he unzipped his sleeping bag just enough to free his arm, and reached for his jacket. Carefully, he removed the binoculars he had wrapped in the protective folds of the fleece lining and set them aside. Then, with one quick, shivering motion, he snapped to a sitting position, shed the sleeping bag and shrugged his arms and shoulders into the jacket. Except for his bare feet, he still wore the clothes he had worn the day before. From beneath a canvas drop cloth that he had used as a pillow, he retrieved a pair of woolen socks, quickly pulled them on, then thrust his feet into his well-worn Wellingtons and grabbed an old hunting cap.

Quietly, so as not to disturb the birds he had come to observe, he opened the back door of the van and stepped out onto the frozen ground. Light snow was falling and sticking wetly to the undergrowth around him and to the reeds at the rim of the lake.

Henry found a sheltered spot next to a crumbling dry stone wall only a few feet from the water's edge and made a dry place to sit by scraping a layer of frozen dead leaves from a large rock. With the earflaps of his cap pulled down and his hands stuffed in his pockets, he was content to stay huddled there for some time. He watched the whooper swans he had spotted the day before as they glided lazily in the frigid water. Several of the pintail ducks had joined them, and this morning there were even a few teals.

Henry enjoyed the feeling of being the unseen watcher—just as he had as a child in the tree house. But after a while it seemed obvious that nothing more exotic than the whoopers and the ducks was going to appear and he began to think of leaving. He had a small twinge of conscience for having deserted Andrea the evening before. And to compensate, it seemed only fair to be on hand fairly early this morning to help clean those miserable Fetherston drawings.

But despite his good intentions, Henry was reluctant to leave. He decided to have one last quick look around through the binoculars before returning to the van.

Slowly scanning the tops of the trees, he spotted several more teals and watched them descend to the water. Lowering his sights and reversing direction, he was surprised to discover a cottage he had not noticed before. It sat back from the lake in a thick growth of brambles not far from where Henry was crouched against the wall. He could see it clearly even without the glasses. With them, he could make out that the small rustic house looked deserted—at least it was in poor repair. No doubt it had been used by a grounds keeper in more affluent days at Rushwood, Henry decided. Sighting a little to the left, he could make out the rear ends of two cars parked on a narrow strip where the road ended. The top of one's license plate was visible, as was the manufacturer's insignia: Jaguar. The other was unmistakably the white Volvo.

Suddenly, to Henry's surprise, the door of the cottage opened and a man stepped out onto the porch. The collar of his coat was pulled up around his ears and Henry could not see his face, until he turned toward the lake.

As so often happens when watching someone through binoculars, Henry had the uncomfortable feeling that Arthur Fetherston was looking directly into his eyes. Henry's equilibrium was thrown off a bit more when Arthur, still looking in his direction, called out, "India!"

India? How odd! Henry was sure that Arthur had not seen him, and even if he had, what a strange thing to say.

"India!" Fetherston said it again, this time with a note of impatience.

In a moment, a young woman wearing a fur hat and a shaggy fur coat came through the door and joined Arthur.

"Don't be in such a rush," the girl said.

"India, my sweet, we really must go."

Henry almost laughed aloud. India was the unfortunate girl's name!

"No telling who will be tramping around here soon." Arthur quickly embraced the girl, then led her toward the edge of the porch. "My bloody brother-in-law said something about 'working' with some photographers out by the lake today."

So, Henry thought, he was not the only liar. Arthur's excuse for not staying to dinner at Rushwood

House the night before was that he had a date in London. Obviously, he had not gone that far away.

The girl stopped in her tracks when they reached the top step and said something that Henry could not hear.

"Oh, Christ! I love you. Now will you bloody well hurry up!" Arthur said.

The girl turned away from him, and for the first time Henry got a good look at her face. It was the driver of the Volvo. She was pretty, with dark hair that curled around the edges of the fur cap and skin that looked incongruously sun-tanned in the setting of the gray, winter day. Her mouth was a lustrous pink with a full lower lip that protruded in a pout. With a quick step, Arthur picked her up in his arms, kissed her and carried her off the porch and out of sight.

Henry heard the girl laugh, the sound of car doors opening and closing, the low hum of the Jaguar's engine, and then the Volvo's, the crunch of the tires, and the excited cries of a few frightened birds that took to the air. Soon, there was silence again.

At least Arthur Fetherston had good taste in women, Henry thought as he scanned the tops of the trees once more through the binoculars.

But then all thought of Arthur or the girl left his mind completely when he saw the flapping of a white wing at the outer rim of the glasses. Quickly adjusting the binoculars, he saw a small swan—smaller than the whoopers—flying low through the light snowfall. It drifted downward on the same wind current as the scattered snow and landed in front of him on the mirrored lake.

Oh, Lord! It was a Bewick's swan! Henry's heart pounded. Slowly, a half-inch at a time, he lowered the glasses and willed himself not to move a muscle. He was so eager not to startle the bird he hardly dared breathe.

He had never actually seen a Bewick's swan before. Still, he was sure he was right. He recognized it from pictures. He had read accounts of its annual pilgrimage. But that it should fly this far south was incredible!

There was no mistake. He recognized the white, white bird with its black bill and black tail feathers and the triangular markings in brilliant yellow beneath the eyes.

A Bewick's swan! Unbelievable! It was a once-in-a-lifetime event, Henry thought. This bird had flown twenty-six hundred miles from its home in Siberia and landed on the lake in front of him! He could have reached out and touched it.

Despite his excitement, his elation suddenly turned to disappointment.

He could not tell a soul what he had seen this morning.

FOURTEEN

AFTER HER encounter with Clayton Foley at breakfast, Andrea was glad to have some time alone in the workroom. She did not like being drawn into the family circle at Rushwood House. Her reason for being there, she reminded herself, was because she was a professional authenticator and restorer of art and she had accepted an assignment. The Fetherston and Foley problems were their own. There was no reason for her to become Deborah Foley's confidante. There was even less reason for her to abide Arthur Fetherston's sticky attempts at flirtation. And certainly, for God's sake, she had no intention of reviving a long-forgotten romance with Clayton. The twanging of her nervous system when they parted in the kitchen was not the result of a chaste kiss on the cheek, but the scent of his after-shave lotion. She had responded not to him but to something that came in a bottle!

She removed the Fetherston drawings from the envelope one at a time and spread them on the worktable.

. . . It was well known that the sense of smell was the most evocative of all the senses. More than once she had been in a crowd—in a theater, a department store, on an airplane—and had noticed the same scent on a stranger. Instantly, Clayton Foley had come to mind . . .

Get to work and finish the drawings, then get the hell out of here, she told herself.

Gingerly, she picked up the sketch of William Gladstone and measured the weight of the paper in her hand. Turning the drawing to the reverse side and looking closely, she recognized the paper manufacturer's watermark. Cecil Fetherston had used an excellent mold-made variety from one of the fine, old English producers of artists' papers. The content was principally linen rags, which had been boiled, shredded, beaten to a smooth pulp, sieved, molded, dried, and pressed.

Under the microscope, the paper had the appearance of a felted or weblike mass of interlaced fibers. The importance of the fiber was the quality of the filelike action it performed. When a pencil, charcoal, or pastel was drawn across the surface, the fibers of the paper acted as files to wear down and hold particles in the interstices. The uniformity of shading that Fetherston accomplished in his drawings would not have been possible on paper of lesser quality.

Naturally, linen and cotton fibers were highly absorbent to liquids. Left untreated, the paper would have had the property of a blotter. To remedy this, and to produce a product that was equally suitable for dry-drawing (pencil, charcoal, or pastel) and wet application (ink or watercolors), the manufacturer added sizing. The effect was similar to that produced by adding starch to a fabric. Each drawing bore Fetherston's trademark—a hair-thin outline of a feather. The sizing material, Andrea decided, was the first consideration in determining the method of restoration.

If she immersed the drawings in a solution as she had planned, the brownish fox marks undoubtedly would disappear—but so would the sizing. She felt certain that the paper manufacturer had used either a weak solution of gelatin or hide glue. She could duplicate his method once the drawings were cleaned. Still, emersion might be unnecessary if a dry method worked.

... She had given Clayton the first bottle of that stupid after-shave lotion herself. It was a joke—a gesture of appreciation—a reward when he shaved off a wiry beard. He liked the fragrance she had chosen for him and wore it every day. There were always traces of it in his clothes. Her apartment—long after he was gone—held a hint of him. Sometimes, when they had been together, Andrea could even smell it on herself.

After they were no longer seeing each other, whenever she unexpectedly caught the scent of that overpriced product from the men's toiletries department in Bloomingdale's, she thought of Clayton Foley. There was nothing remarkable about that, but what she found disturbing was that her thoughts were not just vague memories of someone she had once cared for, but startling scenes of the two of them together. How could an alcohol-based concoction of musk and sandalwood call up images from the past as though they were color slides? Sometimes the mental pictures were so vivid—so detailed and intimate—that they quite took her breath away and left her amazed that memories such as those still ricocheted around in her head...

The sound of the phone ringing in the kitchen startled Andrea. She was glad of the distraction and surprised that she had allowed her mind to wander so far from the Fetherston drawings. After only two rings it stopped. Deborah must have taken the call on the upstairs extension.

With a frown of concentration, Andrea took a box of cotton swabs and two Pyrex custard cups from her equipment bag. Into one of the small dishes she poured a tablespoonful of dry bleaching powder. In the other, she placed an equal amount of hydrochloric acid. After first moistening a cotton swab with the acid, she dipped it into the powder. Particles of the dry bleach adhered to the cotton. While the resultant fizzing action was still going on, she held the swab a quarter-inch above a brownish fox mark in the bottom left corner of the portrait of Gladstone.

The fumes from the combination of acid and bleaching powder had an immediate effect upon the brown spot and it began to disappear. However, a small area surrounding the fox mark reacted, too, and became noticeably lighter than the rest of the aged and soiled paper. The entire surface would have to be cleaned in any case, but there was another dry method that might be more effective.

. . . Memories linked to the sense of smell were not an exclusive conjuring trick of Clayton Foley, she reminded herself. More than once, during the winter season of coughs and colds, she had collided with a hurrying pedestrian who was intent on escaping the blustering wind. Or, she had stood next to someone in an overheated room and come face to face with the ghost of her mother in a whiff of Mentholatum . . .

Andrea emptied and washed the Pyrex cups and stowed them, with the cotton swabs, in the canvas bag. From the clutter of equipment that she had stored under the sink she took a bottle of distilled water and a glass jar that once had held mayonnaise. Measuring a half-cup of water she poured it into the jar and added a quarter-cup of hydrogen peroxide. To complete the simple formula, she needed a quarter-cup of ether.

She reached to the shelf above the sink for the ether before looking. Surprisingly, her hand touched bare wood. When she glanced up, she saw the bottle sitting a few inches to the left of where she had expected it to be. Andrea was always especially careful with ether and had meant to put it well back against the wall to protect it from accidentally being knocked off. She would have sworn that she had done just that. But where it sat now, though not in a precarious position, and only slightly removed from where she felt sure she had placed it, the bottle was definitely nearer the edge than she had meant it to be. Henry must have moved it for some reason, though she could not imagine why.

At any rate, this time, after measuring out the proper amount, she placed the bottle carefully at the back of the shelf.

When she had screwed the lid on the mayonnaise jar, she shook the mixture until the ether solution floated to the top in a well-defined layer. Removing the lid, she dipped a small camel-hair brush into the solution—careful not to penetrate to the water level—then lightly touched the damp brush to a spot of foxing near the edge of the drawing.

...With Aldo Balzani it was different. She had never come across the scent of the Italian glycerine soap he used on anyone else...

"Andrea!" Deborah Foley stood in the doorway between the old kitchen and the new kitchenette. "Why are you up so early? I suppose you couldn't sleep in that dreadful room."

"I slept very well. It's just that I wanted to do a little experimenting."

Andrea decided that her hostess must have been up for some time, too, in order to do her hair and makeup so perfectly. She wore a skirt and sweater the same creamy color as her double strand of pearls.

"*I* didn't sleep very well, thinking about those dreadful letters. I finally talked to Sybil this morning. Clayton called her last night when he got home—even though it was so late—she insists that she didn't send them. Not that there was ever any question. I was sure she'd never make such a mistake. Sybil is much, much too well organized to do a thing like that," Deborah said. "Poor thing, she sounded terribly upset."

Andrea could not think of an appropriate comment, but wondered if Sybil did not send the letters, then who did? Firm in her resolve not to get involved in a family problem, she said, "Clayton told me the mix-up had been straightened out."

"Clayton?" Deborah's voice had an icy little edge, and the look she gave Andrea was more than just questioning, it was almost accusing. "When did you see Clayton?"

"This morning." Andrea was amazed at the glimpse of Deborah's jealousy. "In the kitchen. He told me he had talked to both Putney and the couple from Arizona yesterday evening."

"Of course. You must have seen him in the kitchen when you came down."

"Yes." That's what I just said, Andrea thought.

"You're right, he *did* talk to them, and was able to sort it all out. But still, it's so embarrassing that a mistake like that could happen."

Andrea gave up the attempt at conversation. She laid down the brush she had been using before Deborah came in and picked up a magnifying glass to inspect the Fetherston drawing again.

"I mustn't disturb you," Deborah said.

"It's all right."

"No, you have work to do." She turned to leave, then turned back and said, "Oh. Sybil is bringing the other drawings out this afternoon." The door swung closed behind her.

The brownish mold of the fox mark on the paper was gone, but so was the sizing on the small segment that had been touched by the brush. Andrea concluded that she would try immersion before deciding on the final method of cleaning. It would be a bit more involved and she could use the help of an extra pair of hands—those of Henry March, as a matter of fact.

She was still slightly annoyed that Henry had unloaded the equipment the night before and then hopped back into his van and headed for Oxford. Not that she really blamed him. An evening with his old school chums was bound to have been more entertaining than the one she had spent in Deborah's kitchen.

Andrea poured out the mixture of ether and hydrogen peroxide, then rinsed the jar and let the water run for several seconds to get rid of the fumes.

... If there was a scent or odor that anyone identified with her, she thought, it would not be the expensive Paris perfume she wore when she was not working. The people she knew well would probably be reminded of her by an essence of turpentine, linseed oil, or horsehide glue.

FIFTEEN

INDIA HAMILTON had a sick feeling in the pit of her stomach as she drove past the side road where the van had almost hit her the day before. She shivered as she realized she could have been killed. If the driver had not slammed on his brakes in time, the van would have plowed into the side of the Volvo and she would have been crushed in a mass of metal.

It was not as though she had not seen the van coming. She knew at the time that she had only a split second to pull in front. But she was sure the driver would stop. People always flinched at the last minute.

It was like playing chicken in a drag race on one of those straight, boring highways in Arizona. Afterwards, she always felt sick, just as she did now. But after—never before.

Her mother was right, India did not give a lot of thought to consequences. "Look before you leap, darlin'." Her mother had said that a thousand times. But then Bessie would laugh in a way both conspiratorial and envious, as though she wished she, too, had her daughter's conviction that she would always come out unscathed.

At school, the only thing India had excelled in was gymnastics. Her specialty was the horizontal bar. She took chances that none of her teammates would take, and her flying dismounts left onlookers gasping. She was such a good competitor that her parents hired a professional trainer for her. But India refused to follow the regimen her coach insisted upon. After a short time he refunded her parents' fees and refused to work with her.

In college, she found classwork boring and managed to flunk her freshman year. But one bit of specific knowledge that she did retain came from a course titled "An Overview of Poetry." It was a quote from the Roman poet Virgil: "Fortune sides with him who dares." She believed it, and she lived by it.

As the road widened toward Oxford and she neared the motorway back to London, India suddenly realized she was hungry. Arthur had been in such a hurry to leave the lake cottage at Rushwood that they had not even made coffee.

She stopped at a roadside café and bought coffee in a plastic cup and a sugar bun to eat in the car, then got change for the phone call to her mother.

Bessie answered on the first ring. "India?"

"Hi, Mom."

"Where have you been? Are you okay?"

"Of course."

After something like a sigh of relief or a chuckle, her mother echoed, "Of course."

"I'm just leaving Oxford, I'll be home soon."

"Your father went riding on the Rotten Row horse path early this morning and doesn't know you've been God-knows-where all night, but when he gets back..."

"I'm of legal age, mother." India was aware of the edge in her voice and softened the tone. She could not afford to be defiant, not now—not yet. "You'll think of something to tell him." She always had. "I'll be there in an hour." India hung up. There was no need to hear a lecture over the telephone when she would hear it again when she got home.

A tour bus was leaving the parking lot as India put the Volvo in reverse, then skidded in a turn and sped to the exit lane ahead of it. She left behind a group of angry-looking passengers, a gesticulating driver, and the sound of air brakes as she sped onto the motorway.

Less than an hour later, when she entered the underground garage provided for the town house owners, she was pleased to see that her father's sedan was still not there. Quickly, she locked the Volvo and ran up the back stairs. At the sound of her key in the lock, her mother opened the door.

"I told your father you were sleeping late."

"Thank you." India started toward her bedroom, her mother following behind.

"I don't know what I would have told him if you hadn't gotten home before he did."

"You'd have thought of something." Her mother always thought of a plausible excuse for her daughter's behavior. When India was ten years old and refused to go to school because she had to sit next to the Indian girl whose name came alphabetically after hers, her mother wrote a note to the teacher saying that her daughter had a slight hearing problem and should be moved to the front row. In high school, when India threw up on the front steps of the country club after practically chugalugging a half-pint of gin in the parking lot with her date, her mother explained to the horrified guests standing nearby that the shrimp salad at the buffet was tainted.

The previous spring, when India was caught shoplifting an emerald ring at Goldwater's department store, her parents had made restitution and managed to get the charges dropped. But they were afraid the story had gotten out. To avoid the gossip, the Smith-Hamiltons left for England earlier than they had planned, and took their daughter with them. To anyone Bessie felt called upon to give an explanation, she said that she and her husband felt a British education was superior to an American one, and they wanted India to finish her schooling in England.

The M1 motorway was as close to the campus of either Oxford or Cambridge that India had ever been.

"Darlin', your father is talking about going home." Bessie Smith-Hamilton sat at the dressing table and watched her daughter undress and drop her clothes on the floor of the closet.

"Fine." India pulled out a terry-cloth robe and started for the shower.

"No, wait. I mean all of us."

"I don't want to go back to Arizona." India impatiently leaned against the door to the bathroom.

"I've already checked. They'll let you re-enroll at the university next semester."

"How could you explain that to your friends," India asked sarcastically, "after you brought me over here to get a superior education?"

Bessie was stung by her daughter's remark, but managed a faint smile. "I'll think of something."

"I'm not going back to school," India said with finality.

"Your father thinks it's best. He wants to go home. He's tired of the weather here. And with the mix-up about the Fetherston drawings, he doesn't think they're worth the bother—although I'm sure I can still talk him into buying them if it can be done right away. But he's ready to leave, and he wants us both to go with him."

"You two do whatever you like. I'm not going."

Bessie's cheeks showed a rare flush of anger. "Yes, you are, or you'll have to stay here and get yourself out of trouble for a change."

"What trouble?"

"You tell *me* that. I've been lying for you all your life, but it's been worse than ever lately. You're never where you say you'll be. You stay out all night without any kind of explanation..."

"I'm going to take a shower." India went in the bathroom and turned on the water.

Through the closed door she heard her mother say, "Aren't you ever going to learn to look before you leap?"

India did not answer, but her fingers shook slightly as she reached for a washcloth.

She was afraid this was one time her mother could not help her even if she tried.

SIXTEEN

"I COULDN'T CONSIDER your offer without knowing more about it," Malcolm Putney said to his anonymous caller.

Putney did not usually answer his own phone. His wife acted as his secretary, his financial adviser (most of their money, after all, was inherited from her mother's family), and his research assistant. This week, however, his wife was away. She had gone to visit her widowed father, a provost at Cambridge University.

Thank God for that, Putney thought. All he needed now was for his wife to tell him what her benighted father would do if *he* had received a call like this one. But then, *Daddy* would never have gotten himself into a situation where he had to negotiate for stolen property.

Putney pushed the first draft of his manuscript to one side and propped his elbows on the desk, as he listened intently to the voice of a female caller, who refused to identify herself.

"...it's a drawing signed by Cecil Fetherston," she was saying. "Do you want to buy it or not?"

Though not usually one to inspect the molars of a gift horse, Putney would have given a large part of the advance for his book on William Gladstone to know the identity of the caller. For the second time, he asked, "Who are you?"

"I'm not likely to tell you that, now am I?" Her voice was obviously disguised by a handkerchief or something held over the mouthpiece.

"Why me? I mean, why are you calling me?"

"An act of kindness more than anything else." A fragment of malicious laugh seeped through the filter. "You're not going to sell many of your books without illustrations, are you?"

With as much boredom as he was able to simulate, Putney said, "I might be able to use the drawing you say you have—depending upon the quality—but my book is completed. It's ready to be bundled off to the printer."

That was what he had told his publisher and that was what he had told his wife. In truth, he was becoming more and more concerned that he would never have access to Deborah Foley's collection of Fetherston drawings. Without them, his book would be just another unsubstantiated stirring up of Victorian gossip.

"Come off it," the caller said sharply. "I saw you on the telly last night. It sounded to me as though the Foleys are not going to let go of those pictures at all."

Blast that bloody television program.

"Of course, I could always call those Americans," the woman added quickly. "Smith-Hamilton. Wasn't that their name?"

Putney did not care who owned the drawings as long he could borrow them long enough to have them photographed. But if the Smith-Hamiltons were in a hurry to take them out of the country, it could all get a bit dicey. Trying to sound merely curious, he asked the caller, "Where did you get this drawing?"

"Not likely I'd be telling you that, is it?"

"Describe it. Give me a full description." Putney deliberately fixed his gaze on the tranquil scene outside. His town house looked onto a landscaped courtyard. Snow was beginning to cover the cobblestones and blanket the topiary giraffes that stood on each side of a pump-fed waterfall.

"The drawing is authentic, if that's what's worrying you," the woman said. "It's about ten by twelve—done in pencil and ink."

"Is there a signature?"

"It isn't signed—not his name, I mean. But there's a sketch of a feather in the right-hand corner. I called Sotheby's. They said that Fetherston sometimes used the drawing of a feather instead of a signature."

"Who, exactly, is it a drawing of?"

"How should *I* know? There's no name on it. Except for the feather, there's no identification at all."

"Describe it, then."

"It's some bloke in a top hat."

Putney combed his fingers through his hair and his shoulders sagged in disappointment. He had not really believed that the portrait he was being offered was "The Balmoral Nude," but he had hoped it might be, nevertheless. What this woman was trying to sell him was almost certainly the drawing that had been stolen this week from the restorer's desk at the Victoria and Albert Museum. There had been a story about the theft in the art section of the London *Times*.

"Do you want it or not?"

"No," Putney said. "It's of no use to me."

"Right, then. You've had your chance. I'll call the..."

"Wait!" Maybe he *could* use it. There was no reason to turn it down out of hand. "How much do you want for it?"

"That's better."

"How much?"

"Five thousand pounds."

Actually, five thousand pounds was less than Putney had imagined the price would be, but more than he could withdraw from the bank without an explanation to his wife. Still, there was nothing else for it. He would have to deal with that problem later. "Yes, fine," Putney said. "Yes, then."

"Well done."

"I'll need some time to get the money together."

"It's ten now. You have until noon."

A sudden tremor of nervousness seized Putney. This would be the first time he had been involved in anything seriously illegal. He had done the usual tax-fiddling, a bit of plagiarism, and the necessary misrepresentation of fact that had gone into writing an interesting newspaper column, but this was dealing in stolen property. "I'd rather you didn't bring the drawing here to my home," he said cautiously. "Perhaps we could meet somewhere . . . inconspicuous."

"Get you! I'm not running a bloody delivery service," the woman said. "If you want to buy this picture, be at the call box nearest the main entrance of the central post office on King Edward Street at twelve o'clock. Bring your money. I'll ring you there and tell you what to do next. If you don't answer, I'll be in touch with the Smith-Hamiltons."

He heard the click of a disconnect and the hum of a vacant telephone line.

Putney replaced the receiver but did not immediately move from his desk. He calculated it would take forty-five minutes at the most to get in and out of Coutts' bank and then on to King Edward Street—if he decided to go through with it.

First, he had to consider the consequences. How could he explain having the drawing in his possession?

It was not as though he wanted to lock the sketch away and keep it secretly for his own personal enjoyment. He planned to have it reproduced as an illustration in his book, for God's sake.

One explanation could be that he bought it in good faith, believing it was a newly discovered Fetherston drawing. Or, if that would not wash, he could say he bought it intending from the outset to see that it was returned to the rightful owners, his dear friends the Clayton Foleys. If it came down to it, he might actually give it to them. He could afford to be at least that generous. It was worth taking the risk of making an illegal purchase if it would lead to acquiring the drawing he really wanted—"The Balmoral Nude." The Foley's, grateful at the return of their stolen property, would be less than gracious if they did not happily grant him access to the other drawings.

Access was all he wanted. He could not afford to buy the set. They were not his sort of thing, anyway. His walls were covered with David Hockney prints and two small originals. The decor in his town house was hardly a congenial atmosphere for colorless Victorian sketches. He merely wished to borrow the drawings. He had spoken to Clayton Foley about such an arrangement and thought they had reached an agreement. The Fetherston Gallery—in exchange for letting the drawings out on loan—would get full credit in his book, which could be of considerably more value than an outright sale, and Foley could keep the drawings. That was the argument Putney had put forth, and that was what he thought their agreement had been. Then, last night, Foley had called and said the letter from the gallery had been sent by mistake—even though he still found Putney's offer attractive. Foley had added that they would talk about it again, soon.

Why was Foley hedging? Was he on the verge of making a deal with the Smith-Hamiltons? Well, the woman on the phone had managed to steal *one* drawing. When he talked with her at noon, they would have something further to discuss.

There was one bright spot in this entire mess, Putney consoled himself. He at least would not have to hear from his wife about what he *should* have done. Not quite yet; not until she returned to London. There was no chance that she had seen the Mandy Carruthers program at her father's home in Cambridge. The expensive television set in the mahogany console they had given the provost sat in a corner of his study, picture tube to the wall, a repository for outdated journals and literary quarterlies. *Daddy* had thanked them for the gift, then pronounced it a failure as both a communications medium and as furniture. "Can't get my teeth into anything I see on it—can't get my knees under it to use it as a desk."

Unfortunately, Putney's publisher *had* seen "The Art Beat of London." His call immediately after the program had begun with, "Goddammit, Malcolm old chap, do you have those illustrations or not? Your whole bloody book is nothing but warmed-over stew if you don't have those pictures to give it a new slant." He had said quite a lot more, and it had taken some fancy footwork on Putney's part to step around the questions Mandy Carruthers's program had raised. As usual, when all else failed, Putney came up with a reassuring creative lie that "all was well."

Now, he strode into the hall and buttoned himself into his overcoat. Draping a beige cashmere scarf around his neck, he tucked one end inside his coat, tossed the other over his shoulder, and turned to check in the mirror that the fringe hung straight.

He started for the garage, but decided it was wiser not to drive his own car. A Rolls-Royce got a few second looks even in Belgravia and quite a few in the area of the central post office. The whole expedition was taking on a furtiveness that he was beginning to enjoy.

Hunching into the light snow and cold wind, Putney kept to the inside of the sidewalk to avoid the muddy slush thrown up by the wheels of passing automobiles. At the corner of Knightsbridge and Wilton Place he flagged down a taxi. "Coutts' bank, please. the main branch."

Putney settled into the backseat, smoothing his mustache with his thumb and index finger. By the time the taxi approached Green Park he was relaxed and feeling quite comfortable. As always, he took pleasure in looking at the park.

He especially liked winter days such as these, when the dark trunks and tangled limbs of the trees had the muted contrast of a daguerreotype. The woods appeared so dense through the fog and the flurries of snow as to suggest a forest that extended to the edge of the island, a wilderness that continued unmolested to the English Channel. In fact, it was only about a quarter of a mile as the crow flies, to Buckingham Palace on the other side of the park. If a crow had any inclination to fly on a day such as this—the idea rather caught Putney's fancy—in no time at all it could skim the treetops, perch on the roof of Buckingham Palace and peer across the Mall at the stern marble countenance of Queen Victoria.

The thought of Victoria was suddenly unsettling to Putney. He could imagine her outrage if she knew what he had written about her in his book.

Malcolm Putney had already done a year of research when he began to have doubts about his biography, which carried the working title "Gladstone—Dynamic Liberal." And when he had presented an outline, his publisher was much more negative than Putney had imagined he would be.

"There's nothing new here," the publisher said.

"I plan to go heavy on the fact that Queen Victoria hated his guts," Putney replied.

"It's been done."

"Ah, but not in the first person! I intend to write the entire narrative from Gladstone's viewpoint."

"It's been done."

"Not Gladstone."

"Maybe not, I don't know. But it's been done with historical figures that are much more recognizable than Gladstone."

"Not many people today," Putney said, "know that he was a religious zealot who consorted with prostitutes."

"Who cares? What's interesting about a randy Victorian prime minister? Good God, there's more sensational fare about present government officials reported in the newspapers and on television almost daily."

Putney could not bear to think of a whole year of research going to waste. In desperation, he had suggested to his publisher that he could write a book that concentrated on the same era but had a more sensational character at the center.

"Jack the Ripper," he suggested.

"Been done."

"Oscar Wilde."

"Been done."

"Aubrey Beardsley."

"The sod that drew the men with the really big—"

"He's the one. How about a book on his Victorian erotica?"

"He's been done, too. Several large, profusely illustrated books."

As a final selling stratagem, Putney suggested a general category. "What about—crime. What about, 'Victorian Crimes of Passion'?"

The publisher had ultimately agreed to consider something of that nature, and Putney had left the office with nothing but the title in mind.

His first bit of digging had been done in the *London Times* archives. It was there that he came upon the story of Cecil Fetherston. He pieced together the information about the artist's passion for Emma, the prostitute-model whom he had murdered when he found her in bed with another man. To Putney's great surprise and astonished delight, he discovered that his hero, William Gladstone, had been an eyewitness to that crime of passion.

His research had led Putney to visit the Fetherston Art Gallery. The recently uncovered Fetherston drawings, which were shown to him by the artist's descendant, Deborah Foley—the owner of the gallery—had filled in the gaps in his original research.

It was a story that had *not* been told before, and it all fit together—the drama of Gladstone, Fetherston, Queen Victoria and her beloved servant—lover?—John Brown. It all dovetailed. And if it did not exactly dovetail, Putney would bend a few tail feathers until it did.

But he had to have the Fetherston drawings to make his story work. Most especially, he had to have "The Balmoral Nude" exclusively.

AT FIVE BEFORE TWELVE, Putney stood inside the call box nearest the door of the central London post office. When the phone rang at exactly noon, he answered.

"Putney?"

"Yes."

"Good show," the anonymous caller said.

"What now?"

"Is the currency in an envelope?"

"Yes."

"Fine. Seal the envelope and write this name on the front. Mavis Bell. M-a-v-i-s Bell. I rather like the name, don't you?"

"To what address?"

"Just mark it *To be called for*, London Chief Post Office, King Edward Street, EC1. I'll claim it from the poste restante window."

"How do I get the drawing?"

"The same way. It's waiting for you. All you have to do is show the postal clerk some identification to claim it."

Putney was speechless for a moment. It was so simple. If he dared, he *could* claim his parcel without giving up the envelope with the money.

"And Putney," the woman said, "you can see inside the lobby from where you are, can't you?"

"Yes." He turned to glance through the door at the queues of people at each of the windows.

"It's crowded, isn't it?"

"Yes."

"One of those people could easily be one of my friends, so it would not be wise for you to go off the routine."

"I see."

"Just so we understand each other. Well, it's been a pleasure doing business with you."

"Wait," Putney said quickly before she could hang up. "There's one other thing. I'm buying this drawing even though it's of very little value to me. But there is one of this set I'd be willing to pay more for. It's a drawing of a nude man with a nude woman sitting on his lap. Do you think you could get that one for me?"

"You've taken to a life of crime rather quickly, haven't you?"

"Just answer my question."

"Let's see how this goes and I'll ring you later," she said just before the click of the receiver.

Putney followed the woman's instructions exactly. With shaking fingers he handed the bored postal employee his passport for identification. "Would you check and see if there is a parcel addressed to me?"

The wait seemed interminable while the clerk searched the "to be called for" section somewhere in the back of the building. But when he returned, he was carrying a large manila envelope with Putney's name clearly printed on the front. Unsealing the envelope, Putney quickly checked to make sure that the drawing was inside.

"Anything else?" The postal clerk handed back the passport.

Putney scanned the faces of the other people standing nearby. There was no one he recognized, and no one seemed to be watching him, except for a teenaged girl with a knapsack who was behind him and impatient to have her turn at the window. For a moment he thought of leaving and taking his money with him. But if he was to have any future dealings with his caller, this first transaction had to be completed the way she had planned. "Yes," he said, "I'd like to post this," and he laid the envelope addressed to Mavis Bell on the counter.

Outside, hailing a taxi again, Putney felt a strange exhilaration, as though he had just successfully mailed a letter bomb or sent off secrets of the Commonwealth to the enemy. All together, the sensation was rather pleasant.

FULL PARTICULARS of all British post office services are given in the *Post Office Guide* published annually in November.

The following information is printed under the heading *Post Restante:*

Correspondence marked "poste restante" or "to be called for" may be addressed to the London Chief Office or to any branch office. Proof of identity is required before letters are given up to the addressee. Letters are kept for a fortnight.

When a fortnight had passed, no one identifying herself as Mavis Bell had come to collect the packet. That had never been the woman's intention. She had no legal identification by that name at any rate. She found it amusing that Putney had actually paid for the drawing, which—if anything went according to plan—would implicate him in something far more serious than theft of a rather ordinary sketch.

SEVENTEEN

"I HAVE A GOOD EYE for what will sell," Sybil Forbes said to Andrea. "But I wouldn't like doing what you do—restoration and the lot. I know the trends and the market, and I know how much a painting will sell for. I'm good with profit-and-loss sheets."

Andrea smiled. "I understand you've done quite well with the profit side for the Fetherston Gallery."

"A bit of luck, really, my being there at all." Sybil hefted a large portfolio containing the remaining Cecil Fetherston drawings onto the worktable. "Oh, I have the art background and the business management training, but after a few years as an assistant manager in a gallery that was going nowhere, I decided to give up on the art world. I had gone to manage a small, pricey hotel that belongs to my aunt in Bath, when I met Deborah and Clayton. They were guests there and we got talking. You know how that sort of thing happens. They needed a manager, and I wanted to come to London."

Sybil looked younger than she had appeared on television. Andrea had thought her to be in her mid-thirties. In person, she looked a good ten years younger. The smudged-charcoal coloration around her eyes was less pronounced and rather exotic now, but it was her hairstyle that truly made the difference. Her hair was dark brown and springy with unruly strands that fell loosely to her shoulder on one side and was bunched against her neck inside the high Persian lamb collar of her leather coat on the other. Andrea supposed the French twist she

had worn before was her professional hairdo. No doubt
its severity was meant to strike the note of authority she
felt appropriate for the manager of an expensive art
gallery.

"Deborah says you were the one who first came
across the Fetherston sketches," Andrea said.

"Yes, I was taking inventory. God knows how long
it had been since anyone had bothered. It wasn't so
much the quality of the drawings, but the signature and
the dates struck me as important. I mean, it seemed
certain that it was the work of the original owner of the
gallery, and if nothing else, it would add a nice Victorian touch to the showroom if they were displayed.
Then, Malcolm Putney saw them and started talking
about 'borrowing' them for his wretched book. Next,
Mandy Carruthers caught the scent—I think *she's* the
one who mentioned them to the Smith-Hamiltons and
suggested that someone from the Victoria and Albert
come around to take a look at them. The museum may
be our best customer yet. But, you're not interested in
the business side, I don't suppose."

"I'm interested but not involved," Andrea said. Her
main concern was to finish cleaning the drawings and
to get away from Rushwood as quickly as possible.

"Andrea, love," Henry March said as he came
banging in through the outside door of the old kitchen
carrying a large plaster-of-Paris slab to be used for drying the drawings once they had been immersed in the
cleaning solution. "Do you need this bloody thing or
not?"

"Lean it against the wall for now," Andrea said. She
made a quick introduction of Henry to Sybil. The former responded with the same look of appraisal he gave
the more attractive female art students who frequented

the corridors of the V & A; the latter, with subdued disdain.

"Good. I suppose it's just as well there are two of you here," Sybil said, unlatching the portfolio and extracting a typewritten sheet of paper. "I am delivering the remaining drawings. And I'd like you to be witnesses as I check them off. Then, if you both would sign the list when I've finished . . ."

"Of course." Andrea was a bit surprised at the request. But she and Henry watched silently as Sybil spread the portfolio open on the table and carefully moved the drawings from the left side to the right, counting them out aloud, and checking them off the list as she did.

As she transferred the last one, Sybil said with finality, "Now if you would just sign the bottom of this sheet."

Andrea and Henry complied.

"I've felt it was important to keep track of things ever since someone tried to break into the gallery," Sybil continued, "and, of course, one of the drawings *has* been stolen . . ."

"From my desk," Andrea said.

"Yes, that's true, of course," Sybil said matter-of-factly, "but as I understand it, you had the drawing as a consultant at the request of the gallery—or rather at Clayton's request. Deborah told me that you and Clayton are old school chums. So, under the circumstances, allowances have been made. It wouldn't be quite sporting to hold a family friend responsible for theft."

Andrea found herself staring in disbelief at Sybil Forbes. Signing for works of art that she had been commissioned to restore was the usual practice. It was a matter of record-keeping. But no one before had ever suggested that it was for security reasons. Was this deadly serious little twit accusing her of negligence or—worse—stealing?

"I'll be on my way, now," Sybil said. "Since I've gotten this far out of London today, I think I'll pop on over to Bath and call on my aunt at the hotel." She paused at the door. "I'll be seeing you later at the reception, I suppose, Andrea."

"Yes. Henry and I will be there."

For several minutes after Sybil had gone, Andrea busied herself with the chemical bath for the drawings and fumed silently, wondering if she was being supersensitive or if she had been genuinely insulted.

Henry sat on the edge of the table and watched her with an amused grin. Finally, he said, "Miss God-almighty-self-important forgot something."

"What?"

"She didn't take our fingerprints or ask for our blood type."

MANDY CARRUTHERS pulled the sheet down below her chin and wiped the back of her hand across her mouth. With a small groan she turned her head to look at the clock on the bedside table. It was almost noon, but she would have liked to sleep another hour or so. She did not know what it was that had waked her. It could have been a boat whistle on the Thames outside the window or it could have been Martin Wood's snoring.

She looked with distaste at the rather lumpy man in the bed beside her. A long strand of gray hair had fallen across his face, exposing the bald spot it was meant to cover.

Mandy made no effort to be quiet when she got up and went into the bathroom and turned on the shower.

When she finished and came back wrapped in her woolly robe from Janet Reger's, the snoring continued unabated.

Dear heaven, she thought, how am I going to get rid of him. She should never have let him stay. It was not as though he had the final word on whether she got a celebrity talk show or not. True, his input would be considered by the programming department of West End Television. He might even be able to sway things in her favor if a decision were close, but he was only a news director, not head of the bloody department.

Taking a crystal ashtray and a pack of cigarettes from the dresser, Mandy went out to the small balcony of her second-floor condominium. She left the sliding door open hoping that the noise from the river would save her the trouble of waking her overnight guest.

The construction conglomerate that had built the trendy condos in London's dock area along the Thames advertised them as providing "exciting indoor-outdoor living year-round." The provision for being outdoors in the winter was a chin-high plate-glass windbreak around the parapet.

Mandy scrunched into a canvas sling-chair. She crossed her ankles and propped her feet on the railing, letting the robe fall open to mid-thigh.

"Morning, Mandy."

She looked toward a young man standing on a balcony identical to hers one floor up and to the left. "Hello, Nigel."

"You're looking delicious this morning."

"I can't think why."

"You always look yummy, sweetie," Nigel said. "I bought into this complex because it overlooked the

Thames, but the view of your balcony beats hell out of the river."

"Thank you, Nigel."

"Can I come down?"

"Another time."

"Is someone there?"

"Ummm."

"Ah, Mandy. What are we going to do about your sinful ways?"

"Nothing today, dear."

Nigel laughed and disappeared inside his condo.

Mandy ground out her cigarette. It all had to happen soon. Time was rushing out of control. She had the trappings—strange word, that. She had a fashionable condo, she had a fair amount of celebrity, she could have most of the men who interested her or could help her career. Trappings—they were all just trappings. What was the derivation of the word, she wondered? Hunters engaged in trapping unwary animals. To entrap. Did *trappings* come from *trap*? With a chill she wondered if that was what she was falling into.

EIGHTEEN

DEBORAH FOLEY moved the centerpiece from the dining table to the buffet. She stood back to check the effect, then moved the arrangement of pine boughs and white carnations back to the center of the table again. She was beginning to have doubts about everything connected with the reception.

The conventional thing would have been to wait until the drawings were completely restored and framed, then hold a large reception at the gallery in London. But inviting a few guests to Rushwood to see the restoration work in progress had seemed a novel idea. Somehow, Deborah had pictured it as being a more fascinating process. She had not counted on the smell of the chemicals Andrea used, nor had she realized that at this stage of the project some of the drawings would still be wet and all of them fragile without matting. There was nothing for it but to herd the guests into the old kitchen to see whatever it was that Andrea was doing to remove the stains and spots on the paper. There was no problem with space. People would not be crammed together. The original kitchen was almost as large as the drawing room, and Arthur had always maintained that it was the most charming room in the house. It would have helped if they could have built a fire in the fireplace. That always gave a room character. But even without the "no smoke" regulations it would be dangerous to light a fire with Andrea's volatile paraphernalia in there.

Deborah took a quick look at the hors d'oeuvre trays
and the bar that had been arranged by the King's Table
Catering Company. At least she had not planned a sit-
down dinner.

The thing was, even the small reception was pointless now, because she had decided not to sell the Fetherston drawings.

It was too late to uninvite the guests, but she was determined that the reception would not be one of those
interminable affairs that stretched on into the night. The
time on the invitations was 4:00 P.M. to 7:00 P.M., and
attire specified as informal.

Informal or not, since she was the hostess, Deborah
planned to wear a floor-length dress. As she started upstairs, she decided it would have to be the white wool
jersey with the cowl neckline and the gold belt. One
could always fall back on wool jersey when there was no
time to experiment with something new. She hated to be
rushed when she was getting dressed. More than that,
she felt uneasy about the reason she was in such a hurry.

It was all so melodramatic, the whispering and the
insistence on a secret meeting.

"I wouldn't ask if it weren't important. Meet me for
just a few minutes before the other guests arrive!"

Still, it had sounded so urgent she supposed she had
to follow through. The frantic tone of voice was more
disturbing than the words.

"There's something I feel I have to tell you. It concerns"—there had been a hesitation here—"it concerns someone—it's about your..."

"Who? Is it something about my brother?" Deborah always thought of Arthur when there was a suggestion of trouble. Since childhood, she had heard
numerous accounts of Arthur's misdeeds. Considerate

people who said they wanted to spare her feelings but thought she should know "for your own good" had told her such things as: *Deborah, my dear, your brother hasn't been in school for two weeks.* And when the brother and sister were older—*Miss Fetherston, the girl's family has agreed not to file charges in this unhappy situation, but they insist that Arthur seduced their fifteen-year-old daughter.* And just the previous month—*Mrs. Foley, there's the matter of a gambling debt that your brother says he's unable to pay—*

"It's something that also concerns the Fetherston drawings." The whispered words were full of sibilants and sounded like angry insects swarming around Deborah's ear.

"What is it?" Deborah was growing impatient. "What's happened to them?"

"Nothing yet. Where are the drawings going to be displayed?"

"In the old kitchen," Deborah answered.

"I'll meet you there. Everyone's always a few minutes late, so shall we say a quarter till four? There won't be anyone around to disturb us then, will there?"

"No, but whatever it is, tell me now."

The agitated voice, the furtiveness of it all, made Deborah extremely uncomfortable.

"I can't just *tell* you. You'll have to see for yourself." Then, the whispered admonition, "I wouldn't mention this to anyone else just yet." And that had been the end of it.

Deborah did not know what there *was* to mention. But she did not need to be warned to keep quiet about a problem if it concerned Arthur. She had done that for years.

After laying the white dress on the bed, she took a hurried shower, then began the careful smoothing on of her makeup.

Sometimes she wished Cecil Fetherston's drawings had been destroyed by the brownish mold that had invaded them.

Perhaps she should have taken the advice of the representative from Sotheby's after all, she thought. Early on, she had consulted the auction house about the most profitable way to dispose of the sketches. Their suggestion had been an off-premises sale or "house sale." The expert that she consulted counseled that it would be more profitable to conduct the sale at Rushwood—either inside the house or, if the weather permitted, in a tent on the lawn—than in London on the premises of the auction house.

"There's an enormous advantage to the seller in a house sale," the Sotheby's man had said. "Nothing has to be wrapped or shipped and prices are traditionally higher than in the more staid atmosphere of the permanent auction room. Especially, Mrs. Foley, if you should decide to expand the sale beyond the drawings. Let us say that you include some of the Rushwood crystal and silver, a few of the paintings and perhaps some of the furniture, even some of the linens to round it out. People who have always wanted to see inside Rushwood House will come with the idea of buying some small item in exchange for the opportunity to have a look around. A frayed towel with your monogram is much more valuable than a new one from Selfridges. And more than likely, most of the curious visitors will end up spending more money than they had intended. They'll be carting off andirons and Victorian sofas."

The advice had seemed sound to Deborah and worth considering. When she mentioned it, Clayton had objected mildly on the grounds that it would be disruptive to the household routine, but Arthur had been furious. To show his displeasure, he had not spoken to her for three days.

Deborah, as always, had relented under the pressure of her brother's silent withdrawal. But the devastating effect of his silence had grown less and less over the years. His was not the only voice now. Now there was Clayton. She had given in to Arthur's objection to the auction, but another plan—which she suspected he would like even less—was taking form. People *were* curious about the big English country homes, so why not make Rushwood one of the "Open for View" estates? A room set aside to display the portraits of Victorian notables drawn by the original owner of Rushwood should create considerable interest—especially, she decided, if the sordid history of Cecil Fetherston were described in a glossy, expensive guidebook on sale at the ticket booth. The admission charge for touring the house and grounds would very likely pay for the taxes and upkeep. It seemed an ideal solution.

As many times as she had thought of selling the property, in the end she could not bring herself to do it. She felt a responsibility to keep it in the family for as long as it was possible. Once again the irony of her having inherited Rushwood, when Arthur was the one who truly loved it, struck her.

She slipped into the white dress, buckled the gold belt, and brushed her hair one last time. Turning quickly, she looked over her shoulder in the full-length mirror to check the movement of the skirt as it swirled gracefully around her ankles. The wool jersey had a nice flow and the soft drape of the cowl neckline drew attention to her face and hair. She was pleased with her appearance and decided she would have worn this dress even if there had been time to try on two or three others.

As she descended the stairs, she ran through the guest list in her mind. The Smith-Hamiltons—she supposed she would *have* to refer to them as Lord and Lady. India, their daughter, was coming alone—driving over from Oxford. That idiot Malcolm Putney would be here. Mandy Carruthers—undoubtedly in a low-cut dress. Three members from the board of the Victoria and Albert Museum and their wives. Sybil. Arthur said he would be here. Andrea and her assistant—what *was* his name? Clayton had called from the village pub to say his photo session had ended up there and he had invited the photographer and the advertising man from the Harris Tweed account to come back to the reception with him. How many was that? Not many. There was plenty of food, wine, and cocktails for a group that size.

At the bottom of the stairs, sitting near the front door, was the owner of the King's Table Catering Company and Cantonese Take-away. He had been hired to supply the food and to act as a butler. He was perched on a padded bench between the hall table and the bronze umbrella stand. When he saw Deborah approaching, he stood and reluctantly stuffed the paperback book he had been reading into his hip pocket.

The tall, cherrywood clock at the foot of the stairs said twenty minutes of four.

"Has anyone arrived yet?"

"No, ma'am."

Deborah wished the young man had worn a black cummerbund instead of plaid, and that his hair did not reach to his collar. But she was used to "making do" with occasional help in a house that was designed to be run by a full staff of efficient servants. Deborah's solution to the servant and money problems had been to close off all but about one-quarter of the mansion. What remained was the equivalent living area of a generous house in the London suburbs: four bedrooms, three baths, living room (which was still referred to as the drawing room), dining room, kitchenette and all-purpose room (the old kitchen).

"I've never worked at a do like this when people showed up on time," the butler/caterer said. "Part of the game, really, isn't it?"

Deborah did not feel obliged to comment, but there did seem to be a need to exit with some last-minute instruction. She settled for, "You will remember not to use the coat tree but to hang all the wraps in the closet, won't you?"

"Yes, ma'am."

As she started on through the house, she heard the creak of the hall bench behind her as the sometime-butler sat and resumed reading his paperback.

The drawing room looked rather charming, Deborah thought. One nice thing about winter days was that it was dark by three-thirty and one could use gas logs in the fireplace for light and table lamps. The chintz and velvet upholstery of the furniture looked decidedly shabby in the summer when the draperies were kept open and the full afternoon sunlight streamed through.

In the dining room, she again considered moving the centerpiece but decided to leave it on the table. It did show to its best advantage between the tall, double candelabra. The table looked quite elegant with the ornate silver serving trays and chafing dishes, and with the crystal chandelier casting multi-colored reflections on the white linen tablecloth.

The other member of the catering team, the owner's wife, was fussing with a can of Sterno under the chocolate fondue. She wore a neat black dress but no apron.

"You may as well go ahead and light the candles when you've finished with that," Deborah said.

The woman nodded without answering.

The kitchenette was a disaster. The caterer's dented pots and pans were stacked in the sink along with cookie sheets that had been used to transport the canapés, stuffed mushrooms, and chicken crepes. Crumpled balls of discarded aluminum foil and plastic wrap were strewn around the countertops and breakfast bar, and something white and slippery had been spilled on the floor—horseradish sauce for the cold sliced beef, Deborah supposed. Disgusted, she hurried through the sturdy wooden door and closed it behind her as she entered the old kitchen.

The room was dark except for the light from a small goose-necked lamp clamped to the edge of the worktable.

The first thing Deborah noticed was a cold blast of air from the partially open outside door.

She had expected the room to be empty. She was puzzled, and at the same time annoyed with the woman who was waiting for her. "Why did you come in the back way?"

"I thought it was better that no one saw me."

"How did you get in? That door was locked!"

"Was it supposed to be? I didn't have any trouble opening it."

"What's all the secrecy?" Deborah felt uneasy. "Why was it so important that we meet before anyone else arrived?"

"You'll see. I have something to show you. Adjust the lamp so that the light bulb is about six inches from the tabletop."

"What?"

"There's not much time. Just do it."

The urgency in the voice propelled Deborah across the room to the table. She bent the flexible metal neck of the lamp until there was a bright circle of light on the flat surface.

Behind her, Deborah heard the rasp of the slip-lock being pulled closed on the door leading to the kitchenette. "What are you doing?"

"You won't want anyone else to know about this when you see what I found."

At that instant, a chilly knot of apprehension tightened around Deborah's heart and lungs. It came from nowhere, and she knew it was not reasonable. Still, it was as repellant as almost stepping on a snail on the sidewalk or as terrifying as hearing a moan in the attic that turns out to be the wind. She assured herself that the feeling was unfounded, and when she was urged to look at a sheet of lined notepaper that was placed on the table in the circle of lamplight, she did.

"There's nothing there," Deborah said. "The paper's blank."

She started to turn away, but the excited voice urged her to keep looking—to look closer—only if she looked very closely could she see what was there.

"I can't see it. I don't see a thing." As Deborah leaned nearer, her head bent toward the sheet of paper, she felt the nearly imperceptible touch of something twisted and silken on the back of her neck. At almost the same time, she was aware of the distinct odor of ether.

She straightened, instinctively turning her head away from the unpleasant smell. But the fumes followed her, and in the fraction of a second that it took to shift her balance, she saw a hand coming toward her face. Deborah felt a moment of astonishment that the hand holding the wad of ether-soaked cotton was wearing a leather glove. Then the cotton covered her nose and mouth.

She was trapped like a swimmer in an underwater tunnel, fighting and floundering to find the end, then desperately kicking to reach the surface. One arm swung out wildly, sending the bottle of ether crashing to the floor. Clawing with all her strength, Deborah dislodged the hand from her face. Her mouth flew open. Shuttering and gasping, she filled her lungs. When she released the air, a scream tried to escape, too, but the passage it had to pass through was closed. A knotted silken scarf was pulled tight around her neck. It crushed a fold of the loose wool jersey cowl against the back of her neck and cut into her bare throat in front, choking off all but a few faint gurgling sounds.

Deborah Fetherston Foley's body tried to rally. It made an effort at retaliation that was quickly reduced to twitching muscles and fluttering fingers. Her last horrifying flash of certainty was that she was slipping into that dark place that had terrified her all her life—complete and endless silence.

NINETEEN

EACH OF THE CLOCKS at Rushwood offered a different opinion as to the exact time. According to Andrea's shockproof, waterproof wristwatch, the tall clock in the entry was five minutes slow, the brass and porcelain carriage clock on the table in the upstairs hallway was seven minutes fast, the mantel clock in her bedroom was two minutes faster than that, and throughout the day she had heard chimes and bongs and pings at random intervals from various parts of the house. Her travel alarm agreed with her wristwatch, and when they said it was four o'clock, she slipped on her black suede pumps, closed the door to her room and started down the hall to the stairs.

Since Deborah had asked her to assist with the reception, Andrea was surprised that her hostess hadn't stopped by for her. No doubt she was busy tying up loose ends. "Drinks first, of course," Deborah had said, "but we don't want everyone getting squiffy." It was agreed that an hour or so after the guests were assembled, they would be invited into the old kitchen to view the Fetherston drawings.

There was no possibility of assembling a formal display with appropriate matting and lighting. None of the drawings had been completely restored. Some had been subjected to the chemical bath and were drying. Three had responded well to Andrea's dry method and were awaiting a second application, and others had not yet been touched—including "The Balmoral Nude."

Deborah had suggested that it would be interesting for the guests to see them "as they are." And she was sure that everyone would find it fascinating if Andrea were to describe the process of restoration, perhaps even given a small demonstration.

"Would that be possible?"

Andrea assured her that, with Henry's help, it would be no problem at all.

Naturally, the drawing of the two nude figures was the one of greatest interest. Deborah was determined that it should be displayed on an easel—which she produced from one of the innumerable closets or cabinets or storage bins in the house.

Andrea secretly thought the style and technique of the Fetherston drawings rather pedestrian. The artist was competent—a good craftsman. But he probably owed the major part of his success during his lifetime to being clever enough to draw flattering portraits of the wealthy and well-placed clients who sat for him. There was not a wart, an outsized nose, or a bushy eyebrow on any of them. His subjects' likenesses were staid and proper and meant to be admired by future generations of their families. For that reason, Andrea was surprised when she saw "The Balmoral Nude" for the first time.

She still had not had an opportunity to thoroughly examine the sketch, but she admired its unique vitality at once. The style was freer, less controlled than the other drawings. There was an eroticism about it, but it was far from being salacious. Pictured was a slightly plump young woman, wearing only a head scarf. She was seated on the knee of a muscular man who also was nude. There was no indication that the woman was being held against her will. She leaned sensuously against the man's chest. Nor did she seem in the least displeased that his hand rested on her bare thigh.

The woman's face, it seemed to Andrea, was clearly that of the young Queen Victoria. The features were the same as those in every painting or photograph. Her dark hair was parted in the center and combed severely flat against her head, as she always wore it. But there was nothing severe in her expression. The heavy-lidded eyes had a dreamy quality. The mouth hung slightly open. The thin upper lip that in later years curved downward in a stern line was contradicted here by the voluptuousness of the lower lip.

The artist had not lavished the same amount of detail on the man's face as on the woman's, but it was clear that he wore a beard and mustache and had a broad brow. The drawing, like all the others in the Fetherston collection, bore the brownish stains of fox marks.

Andrea was halfway down the stairs before the part-time butler looked up from his reading and noticed her. He stood and pocketed his book as she reached the entry hall.

Through the arched doorway, Andrea could see that the drawing room was empty. Obviously none of the guests had arrived yet, but she had expected to find Deborah there. "Have you seen Mrs. Foley?"

"She came down about fifteen minutes ago. Went into the dining room, I think." The open appraisal of Andrea by the man in the plaid cummerbund stopped just short of a breathy whistle. That sort of behavior from a real butler—when Rushwood House could have afford one—would have gotten him the sack with no references, Andrea thought. Still, she found it oddly reassuring. It was nice to know that her well-traveled black knit still got that reaction.

"Thank you, I'll find her." Andrea got as far as the drawing room when she was stopped by the sound of the door chime.

As there was no member of the family present, she felt the obligation of an auxiliary hostess and decided to wait and greet the new arrivals.

"We're Lord and Lady Smith-Hamilton," a contralto voice announced.

Andrea stepped forward and introduced herself, while the Smith-Hamiltons' wraps were taken by the butler for the evening and hung on the coat tree.

"I'm sure Mrs. Foley will be with us in a moment," Andrea said. She led them through to the drawing room wondering if Deborah had heard them arrive. And for that matter, where was Clayton?

The Smith-Hamiltons settled on a couch facing the gas logs. Andrea sat on a straight chair near them.

"You're that little Yankee gal who's been working on those stuffy pictures Bessie's so set on buying, aren't you?" Lord Smith-Hamilton gave her a friendly wink. "Do you think they're going to look any better when you get through with them?"

"They'll look just the same, but cleaner, Lord Smith-Hamilton."

"For God's sake, call us Wes and Bessie. We've been Mr. and Mrs. Wesley Hamilton for twenty-six years. Nobody back home's going to call us anything but that anyway."

Bessie Hamilton laughed. "Oh, yes they will, Wes. At least the waiters at the country club will—and those snippy little girls in India's sorority at Arizona State. I'll see to that."

The sound of male voices floated in from the entry. In a moment, Clayton and two other men entered the drawing room. The delinquent host introduced his companions as the photographer and the advertising representative with whom he had spent the day on a photo session. "We started at the lake this morning, then drifted over to the local pub. And though it was all in the interest of selling Harris Tweed, we did have a couple of draft beers." Clayton smiled charmingly at his guests. "And I'll tell you, Lord Smith-Hamilton—"

Andrea was amused that Wesley Hamilton did not invite Clayton to address him informally as he had her.

"—hot British beer doesn't compare to one of my Arizona special Tequila Sunrises. I'll go rustle us up some."

"That'd be wonderful, Clayton," Bessie Hamilton said.

"Make mine Scotch and water," Wesley said flatly. He turned his attention back to Andrea.

Clayton was not easily shot down or even stunned. "You gents," he addressed his compatriots, "won't mind fending for yourselves, I hope. And Andrea,"— he crooked a finger at her—"would you come help me?"

"Of course."

As soon as they were in the dining room and out of sight of the others, he asked, "Where the hell is Deborah?"

"I don't know. I came down just a few minutes ago myself."

"She must still be in the bedroom doing whatever it is that takes her forever to do to her face. If you'll see to the drinks, I'll go upstairs and hurry her along."

Andrea nodded.

"Thanks." He patted her shoulder in an I-knew-I-could-count-on-you gesture. "You look gorgeous," he said. "I was a goddamned fool to ever let you get away." He turned and left the room.

For a moment, Andrea felt a warm little glow of response. She instantly cooled when she reminded herself that it was *her* telephone that had stopped ringing. It was *his* car that had disappeared from her driveway.

While Clayton was gone, one of the couples from the Victoria and Albert Museum arrived. Andrea went through the formalities and seated the newcomers in club chairs near the fireplace. Mandy Carruthers followed a few minutes later, and immediately perched on the arm of the couch next to Wesley Hamilton who, unabashedly, directed his conversation at her plunging neckline.

Andrea was falling behind in taking orders for drinks and delivering them. She decided that the best solution was to coax the guests into the dining room around the buffet table and let them deal directly with the bartender—the distaff side of the King's Table caterers. She was about to issue the invitation when the door chimes sounded again.

As she started across the room, she was momentarily relieved to see Clayton hurrying back downstairs. Then a growing uneasiness returned when she realized that Deborah was not with him.

The door was opened to admit Sybil Forbes. Her hair was pulled up in a French twist again, but her appearance was softened by a moss-green velvet dress and a necklace of silver discs instead of the jeweler's loupe she wore around her neck at the Fetherston Gallery.

Clayton took the gallery manager's arm and whispered something to her. Andrea supposed that it was instructions to come help her with the guests, as Sybil looked in her direction and nodded.

Before the front door closed, Arthur Fetherston entered, preceded by a stunning brunette in a white satin cocktail suit and an off-season suntan.

"There's India." Bessie Hamilton jabbed her husband in the ribs, partly to emphasize the fact that their daughter had arrived, and partly to divert his attention from Mandy Carruthers.

Andrea's concern was growing. She intended to check with Clayton. If Deborah was ill, perhaps there was something she could do.

"Clayton says you could use some help." Sybil Forbes asked with a lack of enthusiasm, "What can I do?"

"See if you can get everyone in to the buffet table."

As Andrea weaved her way around the guests who had clumped together in the center of the room, a tiny warning assaulted her. Deborah was at the front of her mind, but peripherally, as she moved through the group of people, she gave herself moment-by-moment messages: watch out for the advertising man's elbow, he has a drink in that hand—watch out for the photographer's hand, it's aimed at your rear end—avoid the couple from the V & A, but think of something to say to them later. Who's that talking with them? It's Henry! His jacket looks as if he resurrected it from under the spare tire in his van. He could at least have combed his hair. With all of that thrashing about in her head, it was much later before she really thought again about the scene that was taking place at the front door.

India Hamilton reached her arms around Clayton's neck and kissed him lingerly on the lips. She behaved as though she had not noticed or did not care that anyone else was there.

Clayton grabbed her arms and almost roughly pushed her away. He said something to her very quickly, then stepped back, his composure well in hand again, and smiled as if nothing had happened.

The incident had not gone unnoticed by Arthur Fetherston. He looked as though he wanted to strike them both.

"India, behave yourself!" Bessie Hamilton had been watching, too.

The girl's eyes opened wide and she blinked in the direction of her mother's voice. Arthur took her arm. Her trail across the room was erratic, and she stumbled against the edge of the couch, where her mother had made room for her to sit.

When Andrea reached the entry, a second couple from the V & A arrived, escorted by Malcolm Putney. She had to wait until the greetings and introductions had been made before she could speak privately with Clayton. "Where is Deborah?"

"Damned if I know," he said under his breath.

"I'll go check in the back of the house."

"Thanks. She's done some strange things, but she's never failed to show up for her own party before."

The front door had been left ajar. Through it, the sound of crunching gravel and the flash of headlights announced the arrival of the last of the guests, the remaining couple from the V & A. Andrea hurried away to avoid another round of introductions.

The kitchenette was empty, but she could hear someone coughing on the other side of the baize door. It was a wretching, gagging sound. Andrea pushed through. The choking smell of ether almost drove her back.

The caterer's wife slumped against the wall, her hands over her nose and mouth. Through her fingers she said, "I came to get more soda, and there's blood all over the floor."

Although the woman had turned on the overhead light, at first Andrea did not see anything out of the ordinary.

"She's over there," the woman said. "There!" She pointed at the stone floor in front of the worktable.

Andrea quickly went to the crumpled body of Deborah Foley. Her white wool dress was twisted around her legs just below the knees. The broken glass of the ether bottle lay around her. Blood from a deep cut on the underside of her thigh had soaked and spread through the woolen fibers of her dress, creating a surreal pattern. Another cut on her upper arm had bled onto the floor, discoloring the stones.

"Go find Mr. Foley!" Andrea knelt and took hold of Deborah's wrist.

"I don't know where he is!"

"He's in the dining room. Get him!"

The woman still did not move, still did not take her hands away from her face. "Oh, God. She's dead. I knew it the minute I saw her."

"No, she isn't! There's still a pulse." Andrea shouted, "Now get the hell out of here and get some help!"

TWENTY

AN AMBULANCE had to be summoned from Oxford, some thirty miles away, since there was no hospital in Chipping Codsbury. Fortunately, within five minutes of Clayton's call to the emergency number for the village, a uniformed young constable with paramedic training arrived, as did a plainclothes police inspector.

Andrea had already discovered that the cut on Deborah's arm was superficial and that the bleeding from her leg seemed to have stopped. She was careful not to compound the injuries by trying to move her. And because it seemed obvious that Deborah's deep state of unconsciousness was due to the ether, Andrea tried to get rid of the fumes by pushing the partially open back door as wide as possible and opening the window next to the sink.

The nearly hysterical woman from the catering company had been sent to find a blanket and came back with an ancient afghan that had been stuffed in the back of the hall closet.

The young constable appeared, and he discovered the swelling and discoloration around Deborah's neck. The contusions had been hidden by the folds of the cowl neckline of her dress.

"Bloody hell." The policeman looked apologetically at Clayton. "Sorry, sir. But it's a near miracle that your wife survived at all. Looks like the collar of her dress got in the way and took some of the impact of whatever was twisted 'round her neck."

Clayton had gone white. He seemed to be almost in shock himself. Every few minutes he asked the constable to check and see if Deborah was still breathing.

Andrea was asked to stay, in case the constable needed some assistance.

The inspector instructed the other guests and the team from the King's Table caterers to remain in the drawing room until their statements could be taken.

After making a quick survey of the old kitchen and the area outside the open door, the inspector drew Clayton aside and questioned him quietly until the ambulance arrived.

"Clayton, call me from the hospital." Andrea gave him a hug and a quick kiss as he followed after the white-uniformed attendants loading the inert body of his wife into the vehicle.

"Yes, I will."

"Watch your step there, sir." One of the attendants reached out a hand to Clayton and motioned him to a side seat.

Andrea watched the taillights of the ambulance from the open doorway of the old kitchen. When they disappeared around the corner of Rushwood House she began to shiver. It was partly from emotion, and partly because the old kitchen was freezing cold.

"Here, now, Miss," the nice young constable said, "you'd better wrap up. Have you got a coat someplace?"

"Upstairs. In my room."

Andrea started for the back stairway.

"Stay with her, constable," the inspector said.

Both Andrea and the policeman looked at him in surprise.

Nothing could be read in the inspector's expression. His face would register the same inscrutable expression at the scene of a train disaster as it would at the sight of the first spring daffodil. "And when you get back— Miss Perkins, is it?—I'd like for you to have a look 'round in here and tell the constable if you notice anything that is missing. Mr. Foley said you would know better than anyone else."

It had not yet occurred to Andrea to consider a motive for the attack on Deborah. She had been concerned only with the fact of it—not the reason for it. But it took only a darting glance at the easel to convince her of why the intruder had been in the old kitchen. "Inspector," she said, "'The Balmoral Nude'—a drawing that was here on this easel—is gone."

AN HOUR OR SO LATER all the guests had been excused and the caterers were busily packing up their equipment. Henry March had been sent ahead of the inspector who followed him from the drawing room back to the old kitchen.

"Now then, Miss Perkins." The inspector sank heavily onto a wooden stool in front of the worktable. He was a stout man with watery blue eyes that seldom looked up from the spiral notebook he carried. He gave Andrea a quick glance as though to memorize his impression of her so he could write a description later. Flipping to a clean page, he wrote her name on the top line. "You're an old friend of Mr. Foley's, I understand."

"Yes, that's right."

"Sweethearts, were you?"

"I beg your pardon?"

"You were staying here at Rushwood at Mr. Foley's invitation?"

"Yes. Well, no. It was *Mrs.* Foley who invited me. And I wasn't here as a guest. I was hired to restore some drawings that belonged to the Fetherston Art Gallery."

"Yes, I've got all that." The inspector drew a square at the top of the page, then converted it to a cube. "Mr. Arthur Fetherston mentioned that there had been a previous break-in at the gallery."

"Yes, I believe that was before I came to England."

"And at a later date, a picture from this, ah,"—the inspector flipped back a few pages in his notes—"Fetherston collection, was actually stolen."

"Yes," Andrea added without hesitation, "from my desk at the Victoria and Albert Museum."

"So I was told." The inspector tapped the capped end of his pen lightly against his lower teeth. "You're an American citizen, aren't you, Miss Perkins?"

"Yes, I am."

"Do you travel a lot in your work?"

"Yes, quite a lot."

"You must know art collectors and gallery owners all over the world."

"In a number of countries."

"Do you ever act as an agent for any of them?"

"What do you mean?"

"Say, someone you know in Chicago takes a fancy to a painting that is owned by someone who lives in Paris. Maybe that picture isn't for sale in a gallery, or suchlike. But you, in the work you do, might be able to, ah—negotiate with the owner. Or, discover some way of—parting it from him."

"No, never. I restore works of art, and sometimes authenticate them. I'm never involved in buying and selling."

The inspector drew a triangle.

What did he mean by "parting it from him?" Good Lord, Andrea thought, he made it sound as though she were some sort of art burglar.

"We'll want to see your passport, Miss Perkins."

"It's upstairs in my purse."

The triangle had become a pyramid. "We'll want to know exactly when you *did* get here, and where you've been."

Henry, who had been sitting quietly, suddenly laughed. "They'll probably want to see that tattoo of a sailor on your bum, too, Andrea."

"Henry, don't be ridiculous." What had started as a stern reprimand turned into a nervous little laugh. The inspector's line of questioning did seem totally absurd. Surely, he did not believe that she had stolen the drawings and planned to sell them to some foreign collector. And what was that crack about Clayton and her being sweethearts? Did he think there was some conspiracy between them?

"Constable," the inspector said, "why don't you accompany Mr. March out to his van and take a look around?"

"Yes, sir."

Henry turned back at the door. With a hand cupped around his mouth, he said in a loud whisper to Andrea, "When he opens the back door of the van, we'll find out for sure whether that nitroglycerine bomb is wired the right way or not."

When Henry and the constable were gone, the inspector said, "Your assistant has a strange sense of humor."

"Yes, he does," Andrea said. "But I think he finds your implication that I stole the drawings in order to spirit them out of the country as offensive as I do."

"What we're dealing with is theft *and* attempted murder, Miss Perkins. I don't see anything humorous about that."

"Nor do I, Inspector. I was the first one in here after the woman from the caterers found Mrs. Foley." Andrea felt a wave of nausea when she remembered the shock of seeing Deborah lying on the floor, and the bloodstains on her white wool-jersey dress. "I would think you'd want me to tell you about that."

"Right. Tell me about it." The inspector placed his pen and notepad on the worktable in front of him. Though he did not look at her, he crossed his arms as though he were prepared to listen to Andrea without interrupting.

"Well, the first thing I noticed was the strong smell of ether."

The inspector picked up the pad and pen again. "Forgive me. But about the ether. I believe it was a part of your equipment?"

With a sinking feeling, Andrea confirmed that it was. "I'm always very careful with ether. The bottle that was broken was kept on the shelf above the sink, out of sight." She hurried to add, "Though anyone could have found it there. I think someone *did* move it earlier. When I reached for it this morning, it was not in *exactly* the same place where I had stored it yesterday."

"Please continue."

"Actually, there's not a lot more to tell. I thought poor Deborah was dead, but I checked her wrist and I could feel a faint pulse. I told the catering woman to go find Clayton—Mr. Foley—and get help. I noticed that the back door was partly open. It had been locked. I'd locked it myself. Obviously, someone had forced it. Then Clayton came running in—he saw what happened—and he called you."

Andrea paused, expecting a comment or question from the inspector. When there was none, she continued. "My impression was that some unknown person—a *thief*—had broken into the house, and that Deborah interrupted him, so he attacked her. I didn't notice anything was gone—the picture on the easel, I mean—until you asked me to check. But it is possible that whoever was here panicked, and in his hurry to leave, grabbed the first thing at hand, which happened to be that drawing."

Even as she said it, Andrea knew that was not a likely scenario. Her first impression *had* been that it was a random attack. She had thought that until she discovered that the one thing that was missing was "The Balmoral Nude."

"Now, then, Miss Perkins, I'll tell you what I know so far." The inspector consulted his notes. "The lock on the back door was broken from the outside..."

"Stop there. I haven't been outside the house all day," Andrea said triumphantly.

"Is there anyone who could vouch for that?"

"Of course not. No one has been following me around for the last twenty-four hours. But why would I go outside and break back in?"

"That would not seem logical," the inspector agreed, "except that whoever did fiddle with the lock conveniently left a crowbar in the bushes to make sure we'd notice that it was a forced entry, or at least lead us to believe that it was.'' He continued checking his notes where he had left off. ''Since the driveway and walk are gravel, we don't have any tire prints, or footprints. We don't know about fingerprints yet, but I doubt that we'll find any that are very interesting.''

''Except mine,'' Andrea said. ''There'll be some of Henry's and maybe Deborah's. But mostly mine. I'm the one who's been working in here.''

''That's probably the way it will be, all right. Now, I'm not saying that you and Mr. Foley planned anything together . . .''

''Inspector, I deeply resent that, and it's absolutely untrue!'' Before, Andrea had felt a bit frightened, now, she was extremely angry.

''Well, Miss, it's dead certain that Mr. Foley wasn't involved in the actual crime, because he spent the entire day with two reliable witnesses—the photographer and the advertising man. Still, according to Mr. Arthur Fetherston, the two of you—so his sister told him—had been more than casual friends a few years ago. Maybe that's a motive. But the more likely motive is that you planned to sell the pictures on your own.''

Andrea could not believe what this man with the watery blue eyes was saying. It seemed inconceivable that anyone could suspect her of something so dreadful. Maybe he didn't. Maybe this was just the inspector's peculiar method of questioning. But a faltering little voice told her that from his point of view, what he said made sense in a skewed sort of way.

''There's something about those drawings you don't know, Inspector.'' She tried to sound more composed than she felt. ''They're not very valuable. The artist's name is scarcely recognizable today, and his talent was only a couple of notches above mediocre. The drawing that was taken from my desk might bring a few thousand dollars, and then mostly as a historical curiosity. The one that was stolen tonight—maybe fifteen thousand. Do you really think I would be willing to commit murder for twenty thousand dollars when I usually restore paintings and works of art that are much more valuable? And for that matter, in most cases, easier to steal."

The inspector shrugged as though what she had said was of little consequence. "From what I understand, collectors are a strange lot," he said. "A stamp with the queen's picture printed upside-down wouldn't have any more value, as far as I can see, than the postage printed on it. And my wife wouldn't let me in the house with a picture of some sunflowers in a vase. Yellow and brown wouldn't go with her color scheme. She likes pink. So, I don't pretend to know what a certain person, under certain conditions, would be willing to pay for anything."

The inspector picked up his ballpoint pen and beneath the sparse notes he had made of the conversation, he drew two circles. "The only real facts I have so far are that you had custody, so to speak, of the two pictures that were stolen. And that the ether which was apparently administered to Mrs. Foley belonged to you. For the moment we'll leave out the speculation about you and Mr. Foley, because that's only hearsay. But the most important bit of information I've been able to come up with is that you had the best opportunity to commit the crime."

"Me? How could you possibly think that?"

"Isn't it true, that except for the caterers—and I'll check them out as suspects, too, of course, though it seems unlikely that they would know of any buyers for the missing picture. More than likely, they'd go for the silver. But, except for the caterers, you and Mrs. Foley were in the house alone for at least an hour before the others arrived."

"No, you're wrong. Henry was here." Andrea smiled as she remembered that Henry could vouch for her whereabouts. "He can tell you that we spent most of the day working on the drawings."

The inspector flipped through several pages of his notepad before he came to the one he wanted. "This is the statement from Henry March. 'I left the old kitchen at approximately 3:00 P.M. and went to the guest room assigned to me on the second floor to take a shower and change clothes.' Do you dispute what Mr. March said?"

"No." She couldn't. It was the truth.

"So you don't contend that he waited to go upstairs with you and Mrs. Foley to get dressed."

"No, of course not. I had forgotten that he left when he did."

"Well, Miss Perkins, you can see why your situation is troublesome. I could glue it all together and have enough to take you into the station. But what I'm going to do is ask you not to leave the country until we have a better understanding of what happened here tonight."

The inspector made a few more quick notes which Andrea could not read, then connected the two circles with a curved line.

"If you plan to go back to London, I'll want your address there," he said. "And if you go anywhere else in Great Britain, I'll expect you to notify me."

Andrea had put on her down jacket earlier when the constable accompanied her upstairs. Now, she pulled it tight around her. It felt bulky, and she knew it must look strange with her knit dress and high-heeled shoes, but it was the warmest thing she owned. The old kitchen was still cold. She shivered again, and could not seem to stop.

Even she could construct a case against her with the information the inspector had.

"Let's go up to your room now, Miss Perkins. I'd like to check around a bit, and you can show me your passport."

Andrea was looking at the two joined circles on his notepad when he closed it and put it away in his coat pocket.

What would the circle have become, she wondered? Perhaps he planned to make eyeglasses of them—or handcuffs.

TWENTY-ONE

AFTER THE INSPECTOR and the constable had gone, only Andrea and Henry March were left at Rushwood.

Andrea swept up the fragments of glass from the broken ether bottle. Then, by silent agreement, she and Henry began to load their equipment back into the van. Whatever the final decision about the drawings was to be—and for that matter, who was to make it—would have to be postponed.

When the phone rang, it was like an alarm that shrilled a warning in the quiet house.

Andrea picked up the extension in the kitchenette. The call, as she had expected, was from Clayton.

Deborah was in a coma, he told her. That was all that the doctors would say for the time being.

"I'm going to spend the night here at the hospital." His voice was husky with fatigue.

She was still a bit shaken by the inspector's suggestion that she and Clayton were lovers. But they *were* still friends, and she was concerned about him, as well as Deborah. She could picture him sitting alone in the hospital waiting room, so she felt she had to ask. "Would you like me to come and stay with you?"

"No, thank you, darling. I'll be all right."

She could not help feeling relieved.

"Clayton—" She hesitated, but the subject of the drawings had to be mentioned. "I can't stay here at Rushwood. Not with Deborah... Not under the circumstances. But there's the matter of the drawings."

"You can burn the goddamned things as far as I'm concerned."

"How would it be if Henry and I were to get them safely packed away and deliver them to the gallery in the morning?"

"Fine. I think Sybil's usually there around ten."

"Arthur has gone to take the Smith-Hamilton girl home. He said he'd be back later. We'll wait until he gets here so that he can lock up after we leave."

"Whatever you think."

"Clayton—" she was never very good at times like these. All she could think of to say was, "I'm so sorry about Deborah..."

"Thanks."

"I'll keep in touch."

"I'm going to count on that."

Soon after she hung up the phone, Arthur returned in Deborah's Jaguar. Andrea found it difficult even to speak to him. She knew part of what he had said about her to Inspector Chadwick and could imagine what else he had implied.

With as few words as possible, she told him what Clayton had said about the condition of his sister, then she and Henry left.

The drive back to London seemed endless. The motorway was wet and slippery. In the darkness, the taillights of the cars and lorries ahead were like red strobes: passing and retreating, taking curves, occasionally veering toward an off-ramp and disappearing. Freezing rain slanted in front of the headlights of the van and made tiny tapping noises on the front window before being swooshed away by the windshield wipers.

Andrea did not remember Henry's van being so uncomfortable on the way up. The passenger seat was broken, and she had to lean forward constantly to keep it level with the floor.

She was too emotionally exhausted to talk very much, and even Henry was uncommonly quiet.

They had passed the High Wycombe turnoff and were nearing the exit for Heathrow when Henry said, as though he had just solved a difficult mental problem, "Now I know where I'd seen her before!"

"Who?"

"That India creature."

"The Smith-Hamiltons' daughter?"

"Yes. I saw her this morning, right there at Rushwood."

"Where?"

"There's a cottage on the other side of the lake. Did you know that?"

"No. How do *you* know?"

"I went for a stroll in the woods this morning to see if I could discover the pleasures of country life, and I happened to have my binoculars with me."

"So, what about India Smith-Hamilton?"

"I saw her leaving."

"The cottage?"

"Indeed."

"What was she doing there?"

"My guess is, quite a lot—and she'd been doing it with Arthur Fetherston. I assumed they had spent the night in an expression of true love. Then, imagine my surprise when she arrived at the reception and greeted our handsome host, Mr. Foley, with a kiss that all but melted the varnish on the walls of the entry hall. I was hoping to be next in line when her mother took her in tow."

"Henry, you do tend to exaggerate."

"No, it's true. India's mum saw her daughter's warmhearted display and told her to sit down and behave herself."

Andrea found nothing amusing in Henry's observations about India Smith-Hamilton and Clayton Foley. For the remainder of the drive to London, she was even less inclined to conversation than before.

BY THE END OF the second week, Deborah had not regained consciousness. Clayton told Andrea that the doctors hinted that she would never improve. Her heart, her lungs, the functional parts of her body might continue to operate indefinitely. But the thinking part of her brain, the part that separates humans from animals, was a different matter. When her attacker twisted the scarf or tie around her neck, the oxygen supply to the cerebrum was cut off long enough to cause what was almost certainly irreparable damage.

"The doctor gave me a clinical lecture—he showed me illustrations on a wall chart—about how she's never going to get better," Clayton said, "then he shook my hand, gave me a bright smile and said, 'Of course there's always hope, prayer, and the outside chance.' I half expected him to ask me if I wanted to join him for tennis that afternoon."

Clayton had moved out of Rushwood and into the Foleys' flat in London. When Andrea met him for dinner, after discussing Deborah's progress, or rather *lack* of progress, they talked primarily—and impersonally—about their days together at Harvard.

Andrea never mentioned the inspector's suggestion that the events of that evening at Rushwood House had been a conspiracy between them. If the inspector had questioned Clayton along the same lines, Clayton had said nothing about it to her.

The subject of the theft and the attack on Deborah did not come up in their conversation at all. Clayton obviously avoided discussing it. Andrea could understand that. She imagined that he spent most of his time either at the hospital or in some way involved in the investigation. In his situation, she would have needed some relief just to keep her sanity. She looked on their evening together as providing something like that for him.

Clayton did tell her that the only information he could get from Inspector Chadwick was that they were following up on several different leads. He mentioned something about a transient who had been seen hanging around Chipping Codsbury. Other than that, he had nothing concrete to report as yet. "A bit of double-talk, if you ask me."

Andrea was surprised that she had not heard from the inspector again. Still, she had a feeling of foreboding that she would.

Once, she had gone to the hospital with Clayton to see Deborah. When Andrea saw her lying so still and silent, all she could think of was how unhappy Deborah would be if she knew that her hair needed shampooing and that her face was colorless without makeup and waxen in the light from the fluorescent tube on the wall behind her bed.

Andrea's work at the Victoria and Albert Museum was almost completed. She had been asked, however, to stay on and help with a survey of the Royal Victorian art collection. Her part of the project would take her to Windsor and the Isle of Wight.

At first she had refused, hoping that Aldo could get away from his duties as chief of detectives in Florence long enough to meet her at Brighton or Southampton for a few days' vacation.

"I'm scheduled to testify in a kidnapping case in Rome," he said when she called him.

"How long will it take?"

"God knows, darlin'. Come meet me there."

"You'll be busy."

"I'll have to be there when they need me in court, but I'll be free a lot of the time. When I'm busy, you can go shopping on the Via dei Condotti."

"I don't need to go all the way to Rome to shop."

"There'd be the nights."

Andrea did not say anything.

Aldo said, "I'd go from London to Rome to spend one—or better yet, an indefinite number of nights— with you."

Ordinarily, Andrea would have done the same. But she was not certain she would be *allowed* to go outside England. The inspector had told her not to leave. She probably had to be charged with some crime before they could actually stop her from leaving the country, but she was not sure. It was better not to put it to the test. She was afraid she might force the inspector's hand before he found the real assailant.

Finally, she said, "As soon as you can get away, let me know. I'll meet you anywhere in England you say."

"Suit yourself." There was a crispness in Aldo's voice she had seldom heard.

She wanted to tell him about the theft and the attack on Deborah, but not on the phone. If she did, she could imagine his leaving the proceedings of the Roman court in limbo while he stormed into Chipping Codsbury de-

manding that the inspector prove this—clarify that—
and, furthermore, apologize. She liked the idea, but it
was not necessary; not yet. Surely it would all be re-
solved soon. "I love you," she said.

"Yeah? Well, if I don't see you before then, maybe
we can exchange Valentines."

"Aldo..."

"Forget it. I love you, too."

"See you soon."

"Sure." He hung up first.

Andrea turned away from the dead telephone and sat
looking out the window of her apartment at the fine
rain that was sure to turn to sleet by late that night. She
felt she had not been warm since she came to England.
When she complained that her bedroom was cold and
drafty the landlady said, "There's no way to keep the
weather out of this old building, love. But I'll tell you
what I'll do." She left the room for a moment and came
back with a hot-water bottle which she handed to Andrea. "At least this will keep your feet warm."

Drawing the curtains, Andrea glanced back at the
phone. Guiltily, she wondered why she had never told
Aldo about Clayton Foley.

Neither she nor Aldo had ever asked the other for an
accounting of previous real, or imagined, loves. Even
so, she could not think of anyone from her first grade-
school crush onward that she had not told him about—
except Clayton. Why was that? Wounded pride, she
supposed. No one liked to admit that it was the *other*
person who left first.

But that was not true in Aldo's case. He had no
trouble telling Andrea that the reason he had gone back
to Florence in the first place was because of a girl he had
been in love with. They were both members of the Tu-

lane University opera club. The girl was a fair soprano and had been invited to join a small American opera company that was scheduled to tour Italy. They did not need another baritone, so Aldo was not asked to go along. After a summer of being parted from his love, Aldo was devastated. He left school and went to Italy to stay with his father whom he scarcely knew. Aldo's mother had died when he was a young boy. The elder Balzani, in his grief, had sent his son to New Orleans to live with his maternal grandmother.

Aldo's return as a young man to the land of his birth, however, was not inspired by a desire to renew the ties with his father or to be with the countless relatives he had never met. Ultimately, their delight in having him there was the reason for staying. But he had made the journey with a single goal in mind: to find the soprano.

The opera company was performing *Rigoletto* in a small town near Milan when he found her.

"There she was," Aldo told Andrea, "still in her blood-stained costume as Gilda—having just sacrificed her life for her worthless lover. She looked every inch the victim when I surprised her backstage. But as it turned out, I was the one who got stabbed and sliced into tiny pieces when she told me she had married the assistant conductor."

As Aldo told it to Andrea, it had been a wonderful, funny, sad story. So, why had she never mentioned Clayton Foley to him?

The last thing she wanted to do on a cold, lonely night in London was analyze "why."

She went into the bathroom and turned on the tap to fill the hot-water bottle. All the smart money in England must be tied up in some way with the hot-water bottle industry, she thought. A hot-water bottle had been Deborah's solution for a drafty room, too. She had brought one to Andrea to warm the tent bed at Rushwood.

Oh, God, poor Deborah. Who could have done such a horrible thing to her?

BEFORE SHE LEFT LONDON, Andrea wrote a note to Detective Inspector Chadwick telling him where she was going and giving the address of the hotel where she was to stay. A telephone call would have been simpler, but she did not want to talk to him again—ever, if she could avoid it.

Henry March was to be Andrea's assistant once more. He offered to drive her to Windsor in his van, but she remembered the uncomfortable ride back from Rushwood.

"No, thank you," she said. "I'll take the train and meet you there."

The morning she was to leave, Clayton Foley came by a few minutes early to drive her to King's Cross Station. He was carrying two cardboard cartons of coffee and a bag of chocolate frosted doughnuts.

"These are as close as I could find to the doughnuts they used to sell in that miserable coffee shop down by the Charles River. Remember?" He handed her a fistful of paper napkins and, without having to ask, emptied a packet of artificial sweetener into her coffee, the way she always drank it.

The traffic on Euston Road was stalled temporarily, and they were late getting to the station. When they reached the platform, Clayton took her hand and pulled her along through the crowd so that she was almost running. The train was just starting to move when he lifted her onto the step.

She quickly found a seat next to the window and turned to wave at Clayton. It took a moment of scanning the crowd before she found him. He stood smiling and waving back at her from near a doorway that led inside the station.

The train lurched backward a few feet, then slowly and smoothly started forward. Still looking toward the platform, Andrea noticed a familiar figure she had not seen before. Next to the newspaper dispensers—which until the train began to move had been hidden from her view by a broad support column—stood the stout form of Detective Inspector Chadwick from Chipping Codsbury.

TWENTY-TWO

ARTHUR FETHERSTON had scarcely left Rushwood House since the disastrous night of the reception.

Carrying a ring of keys that clanked together as he wandered through the drafty corridors, he unlocked doors and roamed through rooms that had not been entered for years.

In most of the corners there were tangled spiderwebs that still held the brittle outer shells of long-ago devoured insects. Some of the rooms contained furniture concealed by dust covers. Many were totally empty. Some had a chair or two, a bed frame with a dark canopy and no mattress. One quite large room held only a croquet set with two broken mallets and no wickets. There were stacks of sealed cardboard boxes. Some of them were labeled—bedclothes, towels, books, curtains, toys, magazines—and some had no labels at all. Arthur did not bother to open any of the boxes. Whatever they held was of little interest to him.

It was not curiosity that led him from room to room, or even the hope of finding some forgotten treasure. The pleasure was in carrying the keys. As generations of Fetherston men before him had done, now he alone made the decisions of locking or unlocking the doors.

The floors were covered with a thick layer of dust which—it pleased Arthur to note—held the imprint of his footsteps like a plush carpet.

He raided Deborah's store of frozen foods and heated them in her microwave oven. But whether he had a guest or not—India Smith-Hamilton was often there— he ate in the dining room. He used the hand- embroidered linen napkins, the lace tablecloths, and the silver candelabra. After trying first one key and then several others on the key-ring that he kept with him constantly, he was able to open the glass-front china cabinet and use the antique china and the cut crystal as well.

Though he dutifully called the hospital to check on the condition of his sister, he had not been able to force himself to visit her but once. He found the antiseptic smell, the starched white uniforms, and the squishing sound of rubber-soled shoes on the polished floors un- pleasant, but no more than that. And Deborah's con- dition was not an expected shock; he had been prepared to see her in a comatose state. A doctor he talked with had explained that she had not regained conscious- ness—possibly never would.

When he had entered his sister's room, a nurse was adjusting the blinds. She stayed on a few minutes longer to fuss with a vase of flowers.

Arthur felt confident that he was no more uncom- fortable than any other visitor to a hospital patient. He greeted the nurse with a few quiet words and a nod, then proceeded to behave in what he considered a typical manner. Sitting on the plastic-upholstered metal chair next to the bed, he took his sister's hand in his.

"Deborah, it's Arthur. I'm here."

There was not the flicker of an eyelash, the twitch of a finger, the tensing of a muscle.

"Deborah." He paused, and though he knew it was futile, he tried again, with a subject that had always gotten a response. "I borrowed your Jag. You don't mind, do you?"

He might as well have been speaking from behind a soundproof wall. One of his fingers lay lightly on his sister's wrist. He could feel her slow and even pulse. She was not dead—death had its own excusable silence. She was there, Deborah was in there—unperturbed, unconcerned about his presence. Suddenly, Arthur felt invisible. It was as though the still figure on the bed was the only reality, and he did not exist.

"Deborah!"

The nurse turned and frowned at him, startled at the loudness of his voice.

"It's Arthur. I'm here!"

"She can't hear you, sir."

Arthur let his sister's hand fall limply beside her on the bed. He almost knocked his chair to the floor in his hurry to leave. When he was alone in the small elevator that bumped its way from the third floor to ground level, he allowed himself a single jagged sob of frustration.

The power of silence had passed from him to his sister.

THE FETHERSTON Art Gallery remained open despite the incapacity of its owner. Business was no better and no worse than before. With the careful accounting of the manager, Sybil Forbes, and Arthur's artistic advice, it eked out a slim profit primarily from the sale of framed Victorian prints. If the customers—tourists, for the most part—had only known, the same prints could have been purchased for a fraction of the price in the Portobello Road street market at Notting Hill.

After Mandy Carruthers had headed her white convertible Fiat into a convenient parking space at the front of the gallery, she realized she had misjudged the available square footage. There was nothing for it but to back out and find a spot further down the street. The incident should have been merely annoying, but it made another dent in Mandy's confidence. She had been making too many mistakes lately.

She locked the car and had taken several steps away from the curb when she caught herself turning back to make sure that she had not left her briefcase on the passenger seat. Jesus! Calm down, she told herself. You're holding the bloody briefcase in your hand.

She had come to the gallery—after no little debating with herself—to inquire about two things. First, what, exactly, was Deborah Foley's condition. Mandy wanted to know the truth. She had decided that Sybil Forbes, as manager of the Fetherston Gallery and of necessity in close contact with the family, would come as close to knowing as anyone—or rather, anyone who would tell her.

And then there was the other matter—the persistence of Inspector Chadwick. Were his new questions just routine? Mandy had thought the ordeal was over when they left Rushwood that night. Was he continuing to check on everyone who had been there or had he singled Mandy out?

She did not mention any of this when she phoned Sybil for an appointment. Instead, she had told some story about a television show she was planning—a feature on the privately owned galleries in the Greater London area. It was not a bad idea for a program. She might even have done it. Except, "The Art Beat of London" was being cancelled at the end of the month due to budget cuts in public service programming.

Lately, nothing was going well for Mandy.

A tinkling bell attached to the door of the gallery announced her entry. A rather angular young man behind the counter looked up from an American Express card receipt he was filling in for a young man and woman in matching Texas Christian University jackets.

"Be with you in a moment," the clerk sang out to Mandy.

"There you are, love," the clerk returned the credit card to the girl. "And the painting, sir." He held up a large package and passed it across the counter to the young man in a way that was obviously calculated to ensure that their hands would touch.

The girl glared at the salesman and took the arm of her embarrassed companion.

Unabashed, the clerk continued to watch the receding figure of the muscular young man until the door closed behind the young couple. With an exaggerated sigh, he turned to Mandy. "Did you notice their jackets?"

"Yes."

"Do you happen to know if Texas Christians are a sect unto themselves, like Roman Catholics or New York Yankees?"

Not in a mood for whimsy, Mandy ignored his question. "I have an appointment to see Miss Forbes."

"And I'm to deliver you to her upstairs." The clerk locked the gallery and led Mandy up a flight of stairs on the outside of the building.

"I get a case of the shivers every time I climb these steps," the clerk said.

"Why is that?"

"These are the actual stairs that that dirty old man, William Gladstone, ran down—" he paused and looked back at Mandy. "Do you know the story?"

"Yes."

Undeterred, he continued. "Gladstone trotted right down these stairs to find a policeman and report that Cecil Fetherston had murdered his little-bit-on-the-side." At the landing before opening the door, the clerk whispered, "And this is the very room where Squire Fetherston done the deed!"

"Thanks for the commentary," Mandy said.

"My pleasure." He turned and went to reopen the gallery.

It was impossible to conjure up ghostly visions of Cecil Fetherston plunging a knife into the bare breast of his teenaged Emma in the present room. For one thing, where the bed had stood was now an L-shaped desk with an IBM computer on it. Facing the door, next to the computer, was an expanse of bright yellow Formica-covered desktop, which held neat stacks of prints and orderly piles of manila folders containing records of bills owed and bills paid. Behind the desk was a waist-high matching console. And the closet—where William Gladstone was said to have been an observer of Emma's carryings-on—now held filing cabinets with neatly labeled, alphabetized drawers. Instead of a curtain, the closet's interior was concealed from the larger room by strands of colored beads.

The beads began to spin and shimmer, setting up a glassy, jangling sound as Sybil Forbes emerged from behind them carrying an armload of folders which she deposited on the desk.

"So, *there* you are." Sybil's stern expression suggested that she had been kept waiting for quite some time.

Mandy knew that she was no more than five minutes late. She warned herself not to get defensive, and was consoled by the thought that if Sybil was in the habit of frowning like that, she would have deep lines around her mouth and those dark, smudgy eyes by the time she was thirty.

"It was kind of you to agree to see me. I won't keep you long," Mandy said. "I know how busy you must be with—well, with Mrs. Foley in the hospital, a great deal of responsibility must fall to you."

"Yes, it does." Sybil's attitude seemed to soften a bit. "There was talk of closing the gallery, but we've been able to cope."

Without being asked, Mandy sat on the sofa opposite the desk. The couch cushions were large, puffy rectangles that one sank comfortably into, and were upholstered in a bright yellow and white tulip print. A matching chair stood adjacent to the sofa, and convenient to both was a Plexiglass coffee table. The floor was carpeted in a soft, white shag. There was something almost eerie about the fashionable decor of the room that so clearly reflected the taste of the building's owner. She felt that Deborah Foley was present and waiting to hear the conversation between the two women.

Mandy shrugged out of her fur coat. She wore a prim, high-necked blouse. This was not a situation in which her usual V-neckline would be effective. She opened her briefcase and took out a lined tablet and a pen.

"I'll tell you frankly that I almost refused to talk with you." Sybil sat in the chair near the sofa fingering the jeweler's loupe at her neck. A pencil was anchored at an angle in the French twist at the back of her head. "After that television program when you brought in those surprise interviews with Malcolm Putney and the Smith-Hamiltons. It sounded as though the Fetherston Gallery was managed by a total incompetent. Someone who couldn't keep track of who purchased what merchandise—or how many times an item was sold."

"I apologize if that's the way it seemed to you," Mandy said, then hurried on in a professional manner, "but the questions I have today are of a very general nature. We're just trying to establish whether the business climate for small galleries in London is favorable or unfavorable."

For the next several minutes, Mandy pulled obvious questions out of the air and pretended to make detailed notes. Later, she could not have quoted any of Sybil's answers, or even repeated her own questions. But when she had filled three pages with scribbled words and figures she returned the tablet to her briefcase.

"Thank you, Miss Forbes. I do appreciate your help." Mandy stood and put on her coat. She could tell by the relaxed way that Sybil Forbes's hands rested on the arms of the chair that some of the animosity was gone. Now, she thought, she must be very careful to seem casual, but concerned. "Is Mrs. Foley's condition improving?"

"No, I'm afraid not."

"Do the doctors think she's going to—" Mandy carefully watched the other woman's face. Through years spent as a television interviewer, she had developed a knack for reading expressions, for supplying unsaid words. "It's so difficult to know the right way to ask," Mandy's voice was laden with concern, "—what's the word one uses in a question like this. Do the doctors think she's going to—*survive* is the only way I can think to put it."

"I really don't know." Sybil looked shocked at Mandy's audacity, and stood to put an end to the interview.

Mandy hurried on. "Such a dreadful, tragic thing to have happened."

"Yes, it was."

"And the police! As far as I know, they haven't come up with anything." Mandy opened her purse and peered into it as though she were looking for her car keys. "I suppose that Inspector Chadwick has been in touch with you, too."

"No, actually not."

"He told me it was just routine, but I understood he was checking on everyone's whereabouts the afternoon before the reception."

"Well, he did contact my aunt. I had been to visit her at the small hotel she owns in Bath. I drove directly from there to Rushwood."

Mandy took a leather key case from her purse and crossed to the door. "And Mr. Foley—how is he?"

"I'm sure he's doing as well as can be expected."

"Thank you again, Miss Forbes. It's been very enlightening."

Mandy pulled out of the parking space, and at the corner, turned into the narrow lane of traffic. She was satisfied that she had gotten confirmation of what she already suspected:

Deborah Foley was never going to regain consciousness. She probably was not even going to survive. Sybil

Forbes would have instantly insisted that her employer was improving, if, indeed there was any hope of that happening.

And, the police were checking *everyone's* where-abouts the day of the reception, not just hers. *No one* would be able to account for every minute. They had all driven to Rushwood, and driving time was a big variable. It depended on traffic, the automobile, and how fast you drove.

A rotund elderly man in a new cream-colored Mercedes pulled up beside Mandy's little Fiat at the stoplight. He tipped his porkpie hat and winked at her. She quickly turned away with a shudder as though she had caught a glimpse of her future through the car window: fat old men with Mercedes, skinny old men with Porsches, hairy old men with Rolls-Royces, bald old men with Ferraris.

As the light changed and she turned on to the Strand, she gritted her teeth and reminded herself that few battles were won without a bloody campaign.

Clayton Foley was her last, best chance. But it was still too early to show an interest in him publicly.

"GODDAM IT, I can't take much more of this rain!" Wesley Hamilton let his yellow slicker fall in a heap on the tile floor in the utility room of their town house. He removed his Stetson and poured the water that had accumulated on the brim into the double sink before carefully centering the wide-brimmed hat on top of the dryer. "I swear to God I'll die of pneumonia if I don't get back where the sun shines."

"You wouldn't get so wet if you'd carry an umbrella, like everyone else over here does." His wife was at the dinette table thumbing through a catalog from Sotheby's.

Wesley snorted. "What do you expect me to do—canter around Rotten Row with one hand on the reins and the other holding an umbrella over my head?"

He clanked two ice cubes into a tumbler and poured in a generous amount of Glenfiddich. "The best thing about this country is the Scotch whiskey." He went into the dinette to join his wife. "Where's India?"

"In there." Bessie Hamilton nodded toward the living room.

Wesley opened the door and looked through at his daughter.

"Shh. Don't wake her," Bessie said.

India lay on her side on the couch next to the fireplace. She wore blue silk pajamas. Her feet were bare, her toes tucked between the cushions. One hand was thrown back and the fingers were tangled in her thick dark brown hair. The flickering light from the gas logs gave her face a rosy tint. Wesley had seen his beautiful daughter sleeping in that position a thousand times. She looked no different from when she was five years old. She still looked brand new and innocent. Of course, he knew she wasn't.

"Seems like all she does is sleep, lately," Wesley said. "What's wrong with her?"

"Shut the door." Bessie closed the catalog and sat back in the chair. "That's something we need to talk about."

"What is it?" Wesley sat down opposite his wife at the table.

"She's pregnant."

Wesley slowly shook his head, then took a long pull on the Scotch whiskey. "Did she tell you that?"

"No. She didn't have to."

"Well, goddamn."

"Yeah. I know."

"I suppose we're lucky it hasn't happened before."

"Yes. I'd say so."

"She's got the same fire in her britches you have, Bessie."

"Yeah, but I never took my britches off for every whipstitch the way she does."

"I know that, sugar. I've been a lucky man." Wesley leaned across the table and kissed his wife on the cheek.

"The thing is," Bessie said, "what do we do now?"

"Well, who is it?"

"Who do you *think*?"

"God knows."

"It *can't* be anyone but Arthur Fetherston. She hasn't been seeing anyone but him since we've been in England."

"How do you know that?"

Bessie looked at her husband in surprise. "No one else has called for her here, and she hasn't mentioned anyone else."

But Wesley's question had brought up a new and disturbing possibility. Bessie was sure that it would not be the *first* time that India was seeing someone her mother did not know about.

"I can't stand that bloodless-wonder myself," Wesley said, "but then I don't have to marry Arthur Fetherston. I suppose it could be worse."

"Oh, dear God in heaven!"

"What?"

Bessie propped her elbows on the table and hid her face in her hands. She had suddenly remembered the night of the reception at Rushwood. "What if it's the other one?" She looked up in dismay at her husband.

"What other one?"

"What if it's the brother-in-law? My God, she was climbin' all over him that night at Rushwood—right there in the hallway in front of everybody. What if it's Clayton Foley?"

"Surely not."

"Oh, Wesley! *Any* woman would go after him if she had half a chance."

Wesley's jaw set and his eyes narrowed. "He's a son-ofabitch."

"I don't know about that but he's *married.*"

"He sure as hell tried *not* to be."

"What are you talkin' about?"

"I think he tried to kill his wife."

"Don't be crazy."

"Do you think someone just happened to be passing by and decided to come in and strangle Deborah Foley?"

"Whoever it was came in to steal that drawing, and she just happened to be there."

"Oh, hell, Bessie. You don't believe that story, do ya?"

"Things like that happen, Wesley. They're not necessarily planned. Besides, it couldn't have been Clayton Foley. Don't you remember when the inspector was questioning everyone? That photographer and the man from the advertising agency both swore they'd been with him all day."

"Well, if he didn't do it, he got someone to do it for him."

Bessie Hamilton would have given anything if her husband had not said that. Such a thought would not have occurred to her—just as taking it one step further would not occur to Wesley.

"Sugar, if Arthur Fetherston is not the father of our grandchild-to-be, then I think we better pack up and get home as fast as we can get there," Bessie Hamilton said. "But right now, fix me a big, tall Scotch and water."

TWENTY-THREE

THE SAME GREASY MENU, the same plastic salt and pepper shakers, probably even the same bottle of Worchestershire sauce sat on the table of the dark back booth in the Hammersmith Gardens Grill. There was a new candle inside the squat red-glass holder, and there was one other difference. When they had met there the other time—more than a month ago—he had been here first. Now, she was waiting impatiently for him.

She was in the same jogging suit as before. She had even worn the same sunglasses when she entered, but had taken them off once she was settled in the dark corner of the high-backed booth.

For some time now, she had been sitting alone stirring the cup of coffee in front of her. Every time someone new came in, she stopped and looked up expectantly. But when he finally arrived, he took her by surprise. Her view of the door was temporarily blocked by a lorry driver delivering a dolly-load of Coca-Cola cases. He came in behind the driver and walked toward her next to the wall, out of her line of vision.

"Ah, there you are." He slid into the booth beside her.

"Of course I'm here." She heard her tone of voice and warned herself against sounding peevish. There was too much at stake to risk an argument just because he was late.

He kissed her lightly on the cheek. She turned her face quickly and with a hand at the back of his neck pressed his mouth against hers.

He gently pulled away. "We shouldn't be here," he said softly.

"Do you know anyone in Hammersmith?"

"No."

They were taking each other's lines, she thought. Do you know anyone in Hammersmith—he had asked her the other time they were here. No—she had said. That's why we're meeting in Hammersmith—he had said. Everything was reversed now.

"How is Deborah?"

"A little worse each day," he said. "It can't be much longer."

She did not believe him. People in comas sometimes lived for years.

"We don't have to wait, you know," she said.

"Of course we do."

A sullen waiter wearing a soiled apron appeared to take their order.

"Just coffee," the man said, "and a refill for the lady."

They waited silently until the waiter returned. He placed a fresh cup in front of the man and refilled the woman's spilling some on the wooden top of the table. Wordlessly, he wiped up the spill with the edge of his apron, then went to stand behind the bar again and watch a replay of a soccer game on television.

"There are ways to get into hospital rooms when no one is around." She was aimlessly stirring her coffee again. "It would be easy this time. She wouldn't resist at all."

"That's insane! It's much too risky." He looked quickly around the room. There was no one nearby. He had known there wasn't. Still, he said, "We shouldn't be talking about this in here."

"Then let's go somewhere else." Her voice was pleading. She put her hand on his thigh and rubbed the nap on his corduroy trousers. "I can't stand being without you. Let's go where we can be alone. Let's go where we can be together..."

He took her hand and brought it to his mouth. He kissed one finger and said, "If it had been done right the first time," he kissed a second finger, "we wouldn't have this problem." He turned her hand over and kissed the palm. "You made a bloody mess of it, love. Now, there's nothing to do but wait." He laid her hand on the table and slid toward the edge of the booth to leave.

"No!" She grabbed his coat to hold him there.

He gently tried to free himself but she would not release her grip.

"Let go," he said quietly.

"No. You're not going to blame me." Her whispered words were fast and toneless. He could feel puffs of her breath against his ear. "I did exactly what you told me—I thought she was dead. She *should* have been dead—"

He ground a thumbnail into her wrist. She gasped and pulled her hand back long enough for him to stand and move out of her reach.

"Don't leave me!"

She had not spoken loudly enough for anyone else to hear, but the waiter looked in their direction—probably because he saw the man stand and there was still the matter of the tab.

At the cash register, the man paid and refused the change. He said something that made the waiter laugh as he went out the door.

She had taken the bus instead of driving her own car. Now, outside, she began to run.

He already has what he wanted, she thought. Deborah is out of the way—she's never going to be conscious—that's almost as good as having her dead.

The sidewalks were smooth and uncrowded. When she *did* meet someone coming toward her, she ran out into the street, then back again so that she need not break her stride.

Her breathing was controlled and even.

She repeated the same words over and over as she ran, sometimes saying them aloud, sometimes only thinking them in rhythm with her steps.

He *used* me—he *used* me—he *used* me—he *used* me. I *hate* him—I *hate* him—I *hate* him—I *hate*him. He *used* me—I *hate* him—he *used* me—I *hate* him....

TWENTY-FOUR

ON THE GIANT PORTICO of the British Museum a group of schoolchildren chased each other around the huge columns while scholarly readers, taking a break from the quiet of the Reading Room and still apparently lost in profound thought, strolled the length of the terrace and stared distantly above the children's heads.

Malcolm Putney emerged from the interior of the mammoth institution, blinking in the pallid sunlight, and made straight for the stone steps and the walkway to Russell Street. He had spent the morning in the Reading Room and had managed to find some usable quotes for his biography of William Gladstone. Still, he was less than enthusiastic about the prospects for his book without the promised illustrations, and in particular, without "The Balmoral Nude."

The book was not the only thing that had been worrying Putney lately. He could not decide what to do about the Fetherston drawing he had bought from the anonymous woman on the telephone.

He had meant to give it back to Deborah and Clayton Foley that night at Rushwood. Of course, after what happened, it was impossible. Perhaps he should have told the police inspector. But then, how did he explain that he had not contacted the authorities immediately? How could he justify surreptitiously leaving a packet of money at the poste restante window in exchange for that stolen portrait? What possible excuse was there for that disgraceful exercise at the post office?

Better to just forget the entire episode, he had decided. He made a *special* effort to forget that he told the woman there was another picture he wanted her to get for him. She seemed to know a lot about him. She had known which drawing he meant. Suppose the woman was the one who broke into Rushwood. What if she stole the drawing with the idea of selling it to him, and that the attack on Deborah Foley was the direct result? Suppose—in a *perfectly innocent* way—he was responsible for what happened to her.

Putney turned left at Montague Place and soon found himself at the corner of Russell Square. Except for a few students cutting through to University College, there was no one else about. The sun had managed sufficient strength to dry off the wooden benches that had been covered with snow or ice for weeks. Though it was not warm enough to warrant taking off his topcoat, Putney decided to sit for a few minutes and go over the notes he had made in the Reading Room. He had not found a great deal that his previous research had failed to uncover. Still, every new dollop of innuendo or snippet of scandal could be useful.

Without "The Balmoral Nude" as an illustration, he had very little to support his theory concerning the animosity between the prime minister and the queen. He had put forth in his manuscript that Gladstone was continually denied Victoria's cooperation in affairs of state, because affairs of the heart were where her attention was focused. And, that deep grief at the death of Prince Albert was not her sole reason for retiring from public life to Balmoral. It was a private life with her servant John Brown that kept her in that remote area of Scotland.

Flipping open the cover of a lined tablet, Putney glanced over his notes.

With some editing—which he decided to do on the spot—there might be something useful there.

The first notation—dated March 1866—was a quote from Lord Stanley: "The Queen has taken a fancy to a certain Scotch servant, by name Brown . . . [there are] strange and disagreeable stories . . ." Putney marked through the remainder of the quote in which Stanley had gone on to add: "stories probably not justifying the suspicion to which they lead." No need to weaken the first part of the quote with the last.

Putney's spirits brightened. With a little red penciling of quotations like the edited versions one found in theater and movie ads, not to mention on book jackets, he might have something valuable here after all.

From the queen's own journal, quoted in a private letter, was a reference to Brown in which she said, "So often I told him no one loved him more than I did or had a better friend than me." Delete *or had a better friend than me*. Any reference to friendship could knock the romance theory into a cocked hat.

Putney marked through the unwanted phrase and was pleased with the results. That reads much better, he thought, and Brown's reply can stand as is. Now, what we have is, "I told him no one loved him more than I did; and he answered 'Nor you—than me. No one loves you more.'"

Ah, here's a good one. Putney grinned to himself as he found a notation under the heading "Skittles."

"Skittles" was a Mayfair courtesan who had shared the bed of many London notables. She entertained her friends with stories that the talk of Balmoral was that Brown was "the queen's stallion."

I can quote freely, Putney thought, from Alexander Robertson's pamphlet. He actually stated that the queen gave birth to a child seven years after her husband's death, and that the father was John Brown.

There are records, Putney noted, that Victoria visited Switzerland in 1868. And there *were* rumors that she had gone there to give birth to Brown's child.

Putney did some quick figuring in the margin of his notebook. Victoria was born in 1819; 1819 from 1868—that means she was forty-nine or fifty at the time. That rather cuts into the credibility. But there's no need to point out the fact. Readers resented having dates constantly thrown at them. If they wanted to do their own calculations, that was their business.

He was feeling pleased with his morning's work as he walked back toward the museum where he had parked his car, and then headed home.

In the complex of town houses where Putney lived, there were secure parking facilities on the ground level that opened into a central atrium. Full-grown trees in wooden tubs beneath tracks of plant lights sat in all four corners, and across from the elevator were two facing oatmeal-colored couches. On the far wall opposite the unobtrusive door that opened on to the street was a natural-wood desk for the use of the twenty-four-hour security guard service. A video camera hung above the front door.

It was rare to see anyone except the guard in the atrium. One might run into one's neighbors or neighbors' friends arriving or leaving, but no loitering or soliciting was allowed and it was the guard's duty to dismiss anyone without a specific reason to be there.

For that reason, Putney was surprised to see a rather rumpled-looking man sitting on one of the couches drinking coffee from a plastic cup and reading a newspaper. He was even more surprised when he realized that the man was Inspector Chadwick of Chipping Codsbury.

"Ah, Mr. Putney. I've been waiting for you." The inspector stood, folded the newspaper and placed it on the desk, then pitched his empty cup into the metal wastebasket in the corner. "Thanks for the coffee, George."

"It was a pleasure to meet you, Inspector Chadwick." The guard stood as though he were at attention.

Putney was not pleased to see Chadwick. He thought he had finished answering the police officer's questions, and his unexpected presence here made Putney exceedingly nervous. "What can I help you with, Inspector?"

"Let's go up to your place and we'll talk about it."

Thank God, his wife was teaching today, Putney thought as he unlocked the door and stood aside for Chadwick to enter. He did not want to have to answer her questions in addition to those from the police.

"My office is straight ahead and to the left. We may as well go in there."

Chadwick made a silent appraisal of the neat bookshelves, the Hockney prints, the plaid-upholstered armchairs, and Putney's expensive antique desk. He walked to the window and looked down into the courtyard. "Lord, help us. Giraffes!" he said.

"What's that?" It took Putney a moment to realize what had prompted the strange exclamation. "Oh, yes. The giraffes. We have a gardener who is quite good a topiary, actually."

"Seems to me that a tree should be a tree, and a bush should be a bush."

Putney could not think of a suitable comment, so instead, he asked, "What brings you to London, Inspector Chadwick?"

Chadwick sat in one of the plaid chairs and crossed his legs comfortably. "Sit down, Mr. Putney."

Putney did, but he was offended. What right did this country gendarme have to invite him to sit down in his own home?

"I got a telephone call from a woman—she wouldn't give me her name," the inspector said. "I don't usually give credence to anonymous telephone calls, but what happened at Rushwood House was a very serious matter, and I'm checking out every possible angle. The woman said that you have the Fetherston drawing that was stolen from the desk in the Victoria and Albert Museum." The inspector took his spiral notepad from his pocket. "Was she telling me the truth, Mr. Putney?"

Putney did not have to pretend to be shocked. "Certainly not!" The indignant denial had tumbled out without a moment's consideration. He knew immediately afterward that if he were ever going to explain about the drawing, he had to do it now. But it was already too late, he decided. "That's absurd," he added for emphasis.

"I thought it was just a prank call, at first." The inspector drew an elongated rectangle diagonally beneath Putney's name. "But then I remembered that Arthur Fetherston told me you were very keen on buying the entire collection. Said you were strongly disappointed when his sister decided not to sell."

"No. No, that's all wrong. I never wanted the whole collection." This, at least, was the truth, and Putney took on the wounded expression of someone maligned. "I could have used several of the drawings as illustrations in a book I'm writing. But I couldn't afford to buy them. There was only one drawing that I was particularly interested in. And I didn't want to buy it—I wanted to borrow it."

"That's the one that's called 'The Balmoral Nude,' isn't it? The one that was stolen from Rushwood House the night Mrs. Foley was strangled."

"Yes." Oh, Jesus. Maybe he should have told. Maybe he still should.

The inspector had transformed the rectangle into the neck of a giraffe and added a head and two triangular ears. He closed the notepad and returned it to his pocket. "The woman who called me said that you asked her to steal that picture for you."

"I can't imagine who would make such a horrid, horrid, statement. But it is totally unfounded! Such an accusation is absolutely untrue."

"Then you deny ever having talked with this woman?"

"I just did. And I repeat, emphatically, that whatever she said was pure fabrication."

Inspector Chadwick got up without a word and left the room. Putney could not see where he had gone. There had been no sound of the front door opening and closing, so he had not left altogether.

The man had better not be searching the house without a warrant. Putney would have him up on charges so fast—

"This was just where I expected to find it." Chadwick reappeared carrying a flat package addressed to

Putney, but with no return address. "George—the guard downstairs—told me there had been a package hand-delivered to you today. He said he had brought it up himself. Hope you don't mind my fetching it in from the hallway."

"I don't know what that is." Putney was genuinely confused. "I wasn't expecting a package."

"Would you open it, please?"

Putney felt fairly confident—even curious. He knew that the drawing he had gotten at the post office was safely under the paper-liner in the center drawer of his desk. He reached for the scissors next to his oynx desk set and cut the cord.

"You can probably unwrap it easier if you put it flat on your desk," Chadwick said.

I don't need his advice on how to unwrap a package, Putney thought, but he did as the inspector suggested.

Beneath the brown paper were two large sheets of corrugated cardboard.

"Lift the top one up carefully." Chadwick was leaning over the desk. The two men's shoulders were almost touching.

Putney removed the cardboard. When he saw what was underneath he dropped into—rather than sat on—the desk chair directly behind him. "Bloody hell."

"The woman on the telephone told me you were expecting that to be delivered today." Inspector Chadwick sat again in the plaid chair and took the pen and spiral notebook back out of his breast pocket. "That's the drawing you wanted, isn't it? Isn't that the one that's called 'The Balmoral Nude'?"

TWENTY-FIVE

AT TIMES, Andrea wondered if she were in danger of becoming jaded—if she would reach a point in examining and restoring works of art where paintings would become merely defective canvases slathered with paint, or tapestries merely fabrics in need of patching.

Her assignment at Windsor Castle convinced her that this was not an imminent problem. She was stunned by the incredible wealth of pictures, furniture, tapestries, porcelains, and statuary that had been collected and housed there. Splendid Gobelin tapestries hung in a reception room; there was a Rubens and a Van Dyck room. The royal library held treasures beyond belief including an exquisite collection of da Vinci's drawings and eighty-seven portraits by Holbein!

After seeing the vast treasure house of Windsor Castle—only one of several similar properties belonging to Elizabeth II—she began to have some concept of the tremendous wealth of the queen. Still, Andrea found it hard to equate the exalted personage of the queen of England with the woman described to her by one of the guards.

"She comes up to the dear old castle most weekends," he said fondly. "I think she finds it homier than their place in London. Drives up, she does. Likes to get behind the wheel herself, don't she? Here they'll come—the chauffeur sitting beside her, or like as not in the backseat. If they passed by you on the road, you'd think he was the owner of the limousine and she was the hired driver. And when they pull up and she gets out, you'd still never guess that that little woman wearing the head scarf tied in an untidy knot under her chin was the lady of the house here.''

Andrea and Henry were at Windsor to assist in setting up a new system of cataloging. If it had been necessary to examine every object, the time required would have been impossible to estimate. As it was, the project involved nothing that interesting. It amounted to mountains of paperwork and stacks of computer diskettes.

Because of a midweek computer problem that was not solved until the Friday when they had planned to leave, they worked all day Saturday and half of Sunday. Andrea took the train back to London Sunday afternoon.

As the countryside whizzed by her window, she was still thinking of the countless masterpieces at Windsor. The old conundrum came to mind: If the place were on fire, and you could save only one thing—what would it be? A Holbein portrait—a da Vinci drawing—a Rubens—a Van Dyck? There was no way to make a choice. But strangely, the image that swam to the top of Andrea's mind first was that of a small, amateurish pencil drawing—a self-portrait—of Queen Victoria.

In the sketch, Victoria appeared to be in her early forties. She had drawn her chin a bit too pointed and her hair lacked the luster that professional portrait painters had given it, but the eyes were marvelous. They were sad, shining, and wistful and spoke so clearly of her grief and the loneliness of her widowhood. The plaque beneath its rococo frame stated that it was a page from an art exercise book.

Mentally comparing the technique employed in the sketch with that of the Fetherston drawings she had restored, Andrea guessed that the self-portrait was the product of a lesson given at Windsor Castle when Fetherston was the queen's teacher.

When Andrea arrived at King's Cross Station, the memory of the day she left came flying back. She half expected Inspector Chadwick to still be lurking near the newspaper dispensers. She would have to notify him that she had returned, she supposed. Suddenly, the depression she had felt when she left London was back, and even more intense.

The tempo of the train station on Sunday was slower than on weekdays, and the crowd was more convivial. Instead of a congestion of three-piece-suited businessmen, there were casually dressed groups of laughing young people and tired families returning from weekend outings. Andrea felt totally alone. The kind of complete alienation one feels in a crowd of happy strangers engulfed her.

Dragging her suitcase on a metal trolley and clutching her canvas bag of art implements, she cut through the crowd toward the taxi stand. As she reached the outside door, she heard a familiar voice above the noise of the terminal.

"Hey, Red!" Clayton Foley pushed past two teenaged boys who were tossing a small overnight bag back and forth to the protesting squeals of a pretty blond girl.

"Clayton!" Andrea had not told him when she was arriving. "How did you know—"

She was glad to see him. His fierce hug was awkward and friendly. As they laughed at the resultant tangle of her handbag straps and suitcase handle with his umbrella, Andrea noticed someone watching them.

The jogger was standing alone near a pillar. She wore the morbid expression of a witness to a disaster straining to get a better look.

Andrea thought there was something familiar about the woman though very little of her face was visible. The hood on the jacket of her jogging suit was pulled forward and she was wearing sunglasses. When she realized Andrea had seen her, she turned her head, but did not move away.

The whole incident lasted only a fraction of a second—a tiny impression that popped like a water bubble as Clayton took Andrea's suitcase and began to explain that he had called her hotel in Windsor and was told when she left. He approximated the time she would be arriving, "And here I am."

"First, I want to stop by the gallery," he told her, "there's something there you have to see. Then, we're going to have a steak at the only place in London where you can get it seared on the outside and rare in the middle."

"Where's that?"

"At my flat."

Andrea protested mildly that she had a number of things that needed attending in her own flat as they went through the doors, outside to the taxi stand. Turning her head away from a blast of icy wind, she saw the woman who had been watching them spring past and jump into the taxi at the head of the line.

Andrea waited until she and Clayton were settled in a cab and enroute to the Fetherston Art Gallery before she asked about Deborah.

His wife was no better, Clayton said. She had lost weight, and he had stopped asking whether she would ever regain consciousness. It was obvious that she would not.

Andrea took his hand and squeezed it and did not pull hers back when he laced their fingers together.

How difficult it must be, she thought, to see a beautiful woman like Deborah fade into a frail and unmoving replica of what she had been. Could she hear, could she think, was she aware at all of the world around her? Did she know when someone entered her room or spoke her name or changed her bed? Even if Andrea could have brought herself to ask Clayton those questions, a lump had closed her throat and she did not trust herself to speak. She turned toward the window and watched through the freezing fog as the streetlights were turned on in the darkening evening. Neither she nor Clayton spoke again until they reached the gallery.

"What I have to show you is in the office upstairs." He preceded her up the outside stairway.

Andrea stood shivering while he unlocked and opened the door. He set her suitcase down just inside, turned on a table lamp, then stood back for her to enter.

They were in what obviously had been Deborah's office. It was bright and trendy and reflected exactly her personality.

"What a charming room."

"It doesn't look like the scene of a murder, does it?"

"What are you talking about?"

"This is the room where Cecil Fetherston stabbed his girlfriend."

Andrea wished he had not told her.

"God, I'll be glad to get away from this gallery and the musty stories of wicked old Cecil. Not to mention that gloomy house in the country and the rotten weather,'' Clayton said.

''Get away?''

''I'll tell you about that in a minute. Let me help you with your coat.'' He stood behind her and lifted her hair with one hand and held her collar with the other as she shrugged out of her raincoat. Before he let her hair fall to her shoulders he kissed her neck.

''Clayton—''

''Okay. I'm sorry. I never could resist that spot right behind your ear.''

She moved away from him and sat stiffly on the arm of the floral print chair. He had no right to keep reminding her of when she had been in love with him. ''Clayton, what are we doing here?''

''It's business. Strictly business.'' He gave her a sidelong grin with a lifted eyebrow. It was the same charming expression that looked back at most of London from the Harris Tweed ads on the sides of the double-decker buses. ''This is what I wanted to show you,'' he said, taking a large flat package from behind the desk. ''Come here. Take a look.''

Andrea crossed the room and watched as he folded back the brown paper and lifted the sheet of protective cardboard from the drawing of ''The Balmoral Nude.''

''Where—where did it come from?''

''From Malcolm Putney.''

''Putney?'' The effete writer was the last person Andrea would have suspected of being involved in the theft and the attack on Deborah.

''It turned up at his town house, and Inspector Chadwick was there to receive it.''

''But surely Putney wasn't the one who stole it.''

''He says not. He says he was set up.''

"It *couldn't* have been Putney. He'd have to be insane to think he could steal the drawing and then blatantly use it as an illustration in his book—" Andrea stared at Clayton. His expression was more amazing than the reappearance of the drawing. She could not believe his look of triumph—as though getting a second-rate drawing back was the only thing involved. The crime was not just simple theft—but attempted murder.

"I don't really care who stole the damn picture as long as it's been returned. Especially as I've been offered a very good price for it."

"You're going to sell 'The Balmoral Nude'? Did Deborah agree to that?" Even as she spoke, Andrea knew it was a meaningless question. Deborah could not agree or disagree to anything.

Clayton hurried on as though he had not heard. "The whole bizarre affair could not have worked out better. They want to buy the drawing—which is good news in itself—but better still, they want to buy Rushwood House. Thank God. I can get rid of the white elephant."

"But what about Deborah?"

The look Clayton gave her was one of complete mystification. He did not understand what she meant at all. "Deborah no longer enters into this."

For a moment the room was silent. A car went past on the street below and honked at someone in the intersection. Someone laughed and yelled something to someone else. Somewhere, close by, there was a faint, incongruous sound like wind chimes, glassy and tinkling. Andrea dismissed it.

How could she have forgotten who Clayton Foley really was? How was it that—until now—she had not remembered the look on his face that showed no recognition of anyone else's pain?

Andrea's voice was husky. "Rushwood has been in Deborah's family for generations. She wouldn't want you to sell it. She wouldn't even want you to sell 'The Balmoral Nude.'"

"But don't you understand, darling, Deborah doesn't want *anything* anymore."

Andrea reached for her coat. She had to get out of there.

"Oh, forgive me. That must have sounded very callous." Clayton turned on his magazine smile as though the klieg lights and the camera were in place. "I forgot that you didn't know. Rushwood, the damned drawing, *and* the gallery are all going to stay in the Fetherston family."

"You mean Arthur is your buyer? But I thought Deborah was already more or less supporting him. He doesn't have any money, does he?"

"His future-in-laws do." Clayton took her coat and draped it over the back of the chair. "Arthur and India Smith-Hamilton are going to be married."

"Are they."

"And fairly soon. It seems an heir is expected. There'll be a new little Fetherston to carry on the name and walk the drafty halls of Rushwood. At least, Arthur and old Wes and Bessie happily assume that the little unborn tyke is a Fetherston."

Arthur being married and living at Rushwood would please Deborah. Andrea wished she could know about it.

"Things seem to be working out very well for all concerned." Clayton gave her a variation of the bus poster grin. "I've got to get away from here, Andrea."

Again, there was the faint sound of tinkling glass.

"What do you intend to do about Deborah?"

"I'll find a nice sanitorium for her." Compassion was not an expression he could manage convincingly, so he turned his head away and looked at the floor for a moment in an attempt to convey concern. "Didn't you tell me you were going to Los Angeles when you left England?" He looked back at her.

"That's where my next assignment is, but—"

"You must know a lot of important people in California."

"I know people involved with the museums and some collectors . . . I don't know what you mean by 'important.'"

"Darling, I've got to get away from England."

Clayton went to the window and looked out briefly, then came back and stood a few feet from Andrea. He walked with a pronounced limp. She had not noticed him limping since that first morning when they had breakfast together at Claridge's. My God, she thought, even the limp is phony. He uses it like a puppy with a wounded paw. I'm supposed to pat him on the head.

"I can't stay here," he said. "My status now is the same as a widower."

"No it isn't." Andrea was beginning to find him truly repellent.

"I didn't mean that to sound quite that way. But you know how it is. As soon as a man is divorced or widowed,"—he shrugged his shoulders to indicate that there was no word to accurately describe his situation—"all the unattached women he knows start bringing in casseroles or wanting to mend his socks."

Andrea felt as though she were at a West End matinee. She was fascinated by his performance.

"Mandy Carruthers, for instance, has been on the telephone to me at least twice a day for the past week. And I can't show my face here at the gallery because of Sybil breathing down my neck. I haven't been in since the day before 'The Balmoral Nude' was stolen . . ."

He did not even have the decency to say "the day my wife was attacked"—"The day 'The Balmoral Nude' was stolen" was the only way he thought of it. Andrea couldn't look at him. She had to get out of there.

"Where are you going? Don't run out on me again." Clayton stepped in front of her so she could not get past.

"Clayton, I can't stay here. I want to leave."

"Red. Hey, redhead, think about it. Think about the two of us in California." He put his arms around her and held her so that she could not move.

"Let go of me!" He thought it could start all over again. And she had almost let it.

The coarse wool of his jacket scratched against her cheek as she tried to turn away from him.

"It was never over for me." He was whispering. She could hear the confidence in his voice. He was sure of himself—sure of her. "You know that. I've always wanted you."

He wanted what he thought she could do for him. Her heart was pounding and her protests were muffled against his chest as his arms tightened around her and she felt his hands at the base of her spine, pressing her body against him.

"I want to go with you, Red. It'll be even better this time."

One of her hands was flat against his chest. The other arm was pinned to her side. She jerked her arm free and with both hands pushed against him, putting space between them. "Let me go!"

"No. Not again." He was laughing. "I'll never let you get away from me again."

"But you left *me*, you bastard!" She twisted her head to avoid the mouth that was determined to find hers.

Suddenly, the glassy jangling she had heard before filled the room like a thousand windows breaking. Andrea looked toward the sound—toward the closet.

Standing among the strands of glass beads that were strung across the door as a curtain was a woman whose face was filled with the same betrayal, the same hatred that Andrea felt for Clayton Foley.

The hood of the jacket was bunched around her shoulders. One side of the French twist had come undone and springy dark hair fell loosely across her face covering one of her dark, smudgy eyes.

"No!" Andrea screamed when she saw the glint of the paint-scraping knife in Sybil Forbes's raised hand as she rushed up behind Clayton. "No, don't!" The warning was for Sybil. Whether Andrea actually said it or not, what she meant was—he isn't worth it!

Clayton's face was only inches from Andrea's when Sybil plunged the knife downward into his back, just below the left shoulder blade.

At first, he looked surprised. Then his expression was almost the famous grin. His eyebrow went up, and his lips closed, for a moment, at a rakish slant. But then his mouth fell open and his eyes glazed over.

His arms went limp and fell away from Andrea. She tried to hold him up. But it was all too fast, and he was too heavy. She stumbled away from him as he fell. Somehow, she managed to keep to her feet as he slumped, face down, on the floor.

Andrea could not stop herself from stumbling backward. There was nothing to grab on to—nothing to fall against until she collided with the small lamp table, knocking the lamp to the floor.

The office was in darkness and in silence.

Andrea had no sense of the room at all. She could not remember how the furniture was arranged, or even where the door was.

Where was Sybil? What was she doing?

Blindly, Andrea searched the carpet around her for the base of the lamp. Finally, she clutched it in her hand as a weapon.

Still, there was no sound.

Getting first to her knees and then to her feet, Andrea felt her way around the edge of the table until she touched the wall. Inching along, she kept her back flat against the smooth plaster, afraid of knocking into furniture or becoming disoriented without a point of reference.

She had gone only four or five feet when her fingers touched the wooden doorjamb.

Was the door locked? Had Clayton locked it—she couldn't remember. Reaching to the doorknob, she turned it slowly.

There was the spine-chilling sound of squeaking hinges.

If the door had been pulled open quickly, it might have made no noise. But Andrea tried to slide it open slowly and the ancient fixtures screeched—rusty metal against metal—shattering the silence of the room.

Instinctively, Andrea held the lamp base in front of her for protection; ready to strike out if Sybil came toward her. How would she know? How could she hear footsteps on the thick carpet?

But then, she quietly propped the lamp base against the wall. She did not need a weapon.

Through the open door the light from the street lay in a wedge across the room. Sybil Forbes was sitting on the floor with Clayton Foley's head cradled in her lap.

Andrea stepped out on the landing, closing the door behind her. She ran down the outside stairway into the cold, foggy street looking for a policeman to report that a murder had been committed in the room on the second floor.

JUST AS William Gladstone had done more than one hundred years earlier.

TWENTY-SIX

ANDREA SAT ON the stone rim of the circular lily pond and dug into her purse for the official *Historic Building and Monuments Commission* badge before continuing up the broad walk to Osborne House.

"There you are then, Miss." The lady from the English Heritage Society had pinned the plastic rectangle to Andrea's lapel the day she arrived. "No one will stop you going anywhere you fancy with this on, will they?"

The badge was in a zippered compartment of her purse. The same compartment held her airline ticket to Rome and a note from Aldo Balzani giving her the address and room number of the hotel where he was staying. "Just in case," he was not able to get out of the courtroom in time on Friday to meet her at the airport.

She probably would have been able to delay this part of her assignment with the Victoria and Albert Museum, but she wanted to finish now—to put an end to it.

Osborne House, in many ways, was a memorial to the gloriously happy early days of Queen Victoria's reign, and to sad, reclusive final years.

Victoria and Albert, the prince consort, had built the house together as newlyweds. It had been conceived as an island paradise—a seaside villa. Albert had worked closely with the architect, Thomas Cubbitt (who also built the fashionable London district of Belgravia). The house emerged—Italianate in style with two companilelike towers. It was an ideal retreat for a young couple with a growing family.

Now, Osborne House held many morbid reminders of an ancient queen, who, in her widowhood, had closed out the present and surrounded herself with objects from the past. The part of the house where the queen spent her final years was filled with massive dark mahogany furniture. There were depressing statues under glass domes, marble replicas of the limbs of her infant children, framed family photographs on the walls, desks, chests of drawers, and tables.

In Albert and Victoria's marriage bedroom, which the queen had continued to use when she was at Osborne, Andrea was touched by the poignancy of the ornate fabric pouch attached to the headboard of the bed. She read that Albert had placed his pocket watch in it each night before going to sleep. It was hung there on their first night together in the house, and it was still there when Victoria died an octogenarian widow, having survived her husband by forty years.

Stopping only to pick up a photograph from the bedside table, Andrea hurried on toward the room she had come specifically to see—Albert's private bath.

As she knew it would be, opposite the bathtub was an incredible gift from his wife. It was a painting—well over lifesize—by Anton von Gegenbaur titled *Hercules and Omphale*. Pictured was the lovely queen of Lydia, Omphale—nude except for a head scarf—seated on the bare knee of the muscular Hercules. This, Andrea knew with certainty, was the inspiration for "The Balmoral Nude."

She had begun to suspect the truth when she saw the self-portrait of Victoria on the wall at Windsor Castle.

How the drawing happened to be in the Fetherston collection would probably never be known. Perhaps Victoria had given the drawing to her art tutor to frame for her. Perhaps he had simply seen it in her sketch pad and stolen it.

Victoria had sketched her own sad eyes as a widow in the Windsor self-portrait. In "The Balmoral Nude," she had drawn the dark, heavy-lidded eyes with the same skill, but with a hint of the wantonness, revealing how she felt about the model.

And, he was not John Brown.

The model was the same man as in the photograph Andrea was holding. He had the same broad forehead, and the same dashing beard and mustache: it was Prince Albert.

The signature on "The Balmoral Nude" was not an indistinct drawing of a feather—Cecil Fetherston's stylized mark—but a *V* intertwined with an *R*. Victoria Regina.

Neither Scotland, Balmoral Castle, nor any favored Scots servant had anything to do with the drawing at all.

It was a sketch lovingly drawn by a woman who adored her husband, and thought of him as the man in the bigger-than-life painting opposite the bathtub. To Victoria, Albert was her Hercules.

The appropriate title—had the drawing been given one—should have been *The Osborne House Nude*.

First Time In Paperback

Finders
KEEPERS

ELIZABETH TRAVIS

LOSERS WEEPERS

Hoping to acquire publishing rights to the final manuscript of recently deceased literary giant Charles Melton, Ben and Carrie Porter take a working vacation to his Riviera home. They're shocked to find the masterpiece in sections, each one bequeathed to a different heir. Whoever can collect the complete book will own the copyright—and be guaranteed a financially secure future.

Was Charles Melton an evil-minded scamp who set up this devilish scheme in the spirit of revenge? Or did he simply want all his heirs to reveal their true natures? When two of Melton's heirs are murdered, the Porters begin to suspect that a clever author had stuffed his final masterpiece with secrets—deadly secrets—which a killer intends to keep hidden at all costs.

Ben and Carrie are "two likeable, 30-something amateur sleuths."

— *Publishers Weekly*

AN INSPECTOR NICK TREVELLYAN MYSTERY

HOPE AGAINST HOPE

SUSAN B. KELLY

First Time In Paperback

DEATH IN THE FAMILY

Aidan Hope is bludgeoned to death in his hotel room in the hamlet of Little Hopford. The prime suspect is Alison Hope, the victim's cousin, a brash, beautiful, wealthy businesswoman who inherits sole ownership of a lucrative software business. Alison maintains she bought Aidan out years ago. So why had Aidan suddenly appeared to claim his rights and his money?

Fighting his growing desire for the red-haired Alison, Detective Inspector Nick Trevellyan undertakes the investigation. Alison has no alibi . . . and every reason to have killed her cousin. But as Aidan's unscrupulous past comes to light, and a second body turns up, Trevellyan begins to hope that Alison is innocent . . . although that may mean she'll be the next to die.

"A pleasant diversion and a promise of good things to come."

—*Library Journal*

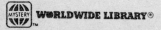

A Sheila Travis Mystery

MURDER

in the Charleston Manner

PATRICIA
HOUCK
SPRINKLE

First Time in Paperback

A LETHAL DOSE OF SOUTHERN COMFORT

"Trouble follows that woman like fleas follow a dog," her father had always said about Aunt Mary. Sheila Travis ruefully agrees when she is dispatched by her colorful aunt to Charleston to "investigate" some mysterious accidents occurring at the historic home of Mary's childhood friends, Dolly and Marion.

Sheila's hostesses are a monument to Southern hospitality, and though a master at protocol, the former ambassador's wife feels boorish by comparison. But this isn't a social visit—Sheila has a job to do even if she's initially inclined to write the accidents off as coincidence. The first murder changes her mind....

"A plethora of likely suspects, all with motives, means and opportunity."

—*Booklist*

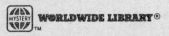

A PORT SILVA MYSTERY

GRANDMOTHER'S HOUSE

JANET LAPIERRE

First Time in Paperback

PORT SILVA—LAND TO KILL FOR?

Situated on California's beautiful northern coast, Port Silva had escaped the rash of land developers eating up the state's prime real estate. But when a posh San Diego firm finally offers small fortunes to persuade the people on historic Finn Lane to sell out, everyone jumps at the chance. Except thirteen-year-old Petey Birdsong. The house belonged to his grandmother. He's not selling. Charlotte, his mother, stands adamantly beside him.

But how far will Petey go to defend his home?

"LaPierre is something else . . . real talent."
—*Mystery Readers of America Journal*

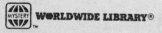

WORLDWIDE LIBRARY®

COFFIN IN THE MUSEUM OF CRIME

First Time In Paperback

A
JOHN
COFFIN
MYSTERY

Gwendoline Butler

MATTERS OF THE HEAD

Life was good for Detective John Coffin—he'd earned a promotion and had just moved into a new home in the tower of a renovated church-turned-theater. True, he now headed his own force and was no longer a street detective, but his business was still crime and there was plenty in the Docklands.

And then a severed human head was found in an urn on the church steps. A hand turned up in a freezer upstairs. It was one of those cases that stretched out long fingers to touch many lives...or, rather, deaths.

"Butler pens a superior procedural." —*Publishers Weekly*

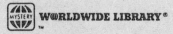